LAZARUS FINDS

by
Tim Megaw

To Louisa, for always demanding the next chapter.

THE END

IT WAS A little after six o'clock when Lazarus Finds, Laz to his friends, drove the short distance from his office at the Yours Mutual building on Market towards his club on Broad. It was a journey he had made many times over the last twenty years or so. Today had been a day much like any other, no more grueling, no less, but Laz could not wait to get that first glass of Scotch inside him, or the first three in fact. He passed William Penn's perch atop City Hall, the Bellevue Hotel, the crowds queuing for the ballet at the Academy of Music and pulled in at the City Park opposite. He handed over his keys to the faceless attendant behind the balaclava and, pulling his own collar up against the incoming December chill which was slowly making its way off the Delaware. Laz crossed the street and headed up the steps into his sanctuary.

"Good Evening Mr Finds" intoned the doorman with enough practiced deference to appear sufficiently welcoming while opening wide the portal that beckoned Laz to finally commence the most anticipated part of his day.

"Um, Good Evening Sloanes, um, Soames" he mumbled back, again reminding himself he really should learn the man's name, but it had been a score or so years and the door still opened each night, so did it really matter? Inside the concierge stood at his desk, ticking Laz's name off a list as he appeared.

"Anyone in?" asked Laz.

"Mr Aubrey is in Sir," came the reply as it had many thousand of times before "I'm sure Mr Richard will not be too long behind you Mr Finds."

Mr Richard was in fact Dick Posman – his best friend, a corporate lawyer also with Yours Mutual, the large Philly-based life insurance company — and Aubrey Fink his other, and only other good friend come to that, Laz thought, a 'Main Liner', who seemed not to be sure where his money came from or how much he had left, but reckoned it would last at least until he ended up dead of a heart attack on the floor of the Brandywine Room in the, perhaps, not too distant future.

The girl from the cloakroom took Laz's coat and briefcase. She didn't bother to give him a ticket, she knew by now that he would only get drunk and lose it (most of them did), rather she put it in the special corner that had been reserved for him for years and hoped he would tip her now, knowing there was no hope of one later. The tip was not forthcoming, rather Laz made his way into the Brandywine Room and sidled up to Aubrey at the bar. "Good Evening Aubrey" he greeted him as usual "tough day spending Grandpapa's money?"

"Much of a muchness" Aubrey responded "can't complain."

Laz observed Aubrey's empty glass. He waited, playing his usual game, to see whether out-of-the-blue Aubrey should offer to buy him a drink, but he knew it would never happen. He couldn't remember whether it ever had. The desire to had something warm and alcoholic inside him, sooner rather than later, quickly got the better of him. "What are you having Aubrey?" he asked at last.

Aubrey studied his glass as if he couldn't remember. Laz could see the vessel had last held water. Aubrey had a different recollection. "Um, it's the 25 year Bowmore, Laz" Aubrey told him, following the lie with a soft gulp half from the anticipation of the drink, half from shame of the lie perhaps. "Lovely drink" he added unnecessarily. Lazarus signaled the barman who wandered slowly down towards them, wiping glasses and tidying as he came.

"Good evening Mr Finds" he began his well worn routine. Laz just nodded and fumbled for his cellphone which was buzzing somewhere. "Crown Royal for you, Mr Finds?" continued the barman. "And whatever Aubrey's having," Laz finished, giving up on finding the phone as the buzzing eventually stopped. The barman looked to Aubrey for a clue.

"It's the Bowmore Twenty-Five…" Aubrey advised, staring the barman down.

"The Twenty Five" nodded the barman. "Of course, Mr. Fink." The barman couldn't actually remember Aubrey having ever purchased a drink in the company of others, neither in fact could Laz, but Aubrey was one of those fellows that Laz had depended heavily upon all those years ago to get in the club in the first place and, in a way, Laz felt he was still paying back those dues. So did many others in fact.

"Good day at the office?" Aubrey asked as the single malt arrived, not that he was particularly interested, but he knew Laz's prolonged and extruded answer would no doubt give him plenty of time to savor the legendary peatiness of the liquid amber he cherished in his palm.

"Usual shit-fest" Laz answered coarsely, because Laz had become exceedingly coarse over the last few years or so, even bordering on the moronic, Aubrey and many others had noticed. 'Fucking Dangle just wants more policies sold, higher premiums, more additional charges bolted on to existing policies… Then I put it to the sales teams, I travel round half the fucking country to drill it into them, and Causley says I'm driving them too hard and they're complaining about me! Me for Christ's sake! What the hell am I supposed to do?" Laz took a deep slug of the whiskey "…and then Zee says we have to be warmer and fuzzier and make a better connection with the clients!"

Aubrey had heard all these names before, for nigh on twenty years or so, but he never really remembered who they were or what they did, nor did he really care to. And as to the content, well the recording never stopped. Oh, the stakes he supposed got higher. It wasn't so long ago Laz would have been complaining about the size of his desk, or his spot in the parking garage or the view from his window, or not even having a window; but it all came down to the same thing. Laz droned on and on while Aubrey nurtured the malt, silently thanking his grandfather for creating a toilet paper empire that made him millions and then having the decency and foresight of selling it long before Aubrey came into the world. Aubrey nodded to Laz when it seemed appropriate, shook his head if the nod seemed to have received the wrong reaction and hoped Dick would arrive soon so he could be gone. Laz got another one in, 'what the heck' thought Aubrey and signaled another one in for himself.

The club had been Lazarus's after work haunt since the time he'd been advised by his wife Mary, not so long after they had been first married and she had passed it along from her father, that if he wanted to get anywhere in the business world in this town he'd better apply to join. He had been lucky in one respect, with his father-in-law's support and the backing of Aubrey, whom he knew from Widener, he had gotten in after a couple of attempts.

In another sense, it hadn't worked. His career had probably suffered terribly from the lost hours spent at the club rather than in his office at Yours Mutual, plus he'd downed tens, if not hundreds of thousands of dollars in Scotch and Single Malt at the bar of the Brandywine Room since the day he was, finally, accepted. Still, if this was going through the motions, then going through the motions he was happy to do.

Eventually Dick Posman arrived in a flurry of overcoats, scarves, gloves and briefcases which he tossed to the coat check girl, along with a ten dollar tip, before rushing into the Brandywine Room. He knew exactly where Laz would be, indeed where he had been most of the evenings they had spent together over the last couple of decades. Dick threw his hands wide apart.

"Laz" he cried "where the hell were you?"

Laz looked up from his Crown Royal, was it his second or third he wondered and why was Dick so late tonight? "Where the hell was I, why, er what?" he asked.

Dick signaled the barman and drew up a stool, "Jesus Laz" he sighed "Director's meeting in Doug's office! Six o'clock! You were supposed to present the next quarter's sales forecasts!"

Laz slapped his forehead hard, so hard he spilled whiskey out of the glass that he held in the other hand. "Fuck!" he shouted, causing several other members and their wives to turn to look and see where the commotion was coming from. Upon seeing the cause, they just sighed or nodded knowingly. Laz shook his head "I totally forgot…"

Dick was wide-eyed, "How could you forget?" he asked exasperatedly "it was your presentation!"

"Fuck" Laz said again "I was on my way there… and then I was here. It completely slipped my mind!"

"Dangle was fit to be tied, absolutely apoplectic" Dick painted the scene while Aubrey signaled for a quick one 'for the road,' "he sent out search parties for you… Causley even suggested calling over here. Then I had your secretary call up and say Stephen had had an accident at school — so you'd better make something good up by tomorrow!"

Laz sighed with the relief of a man given a twenty-four

hour stay of execution, "So we'll do it tomorrow then" he confirmed.

"No, it's done" advised Dick "he called in Leanne, she gave the presentation. It went very well"

"He called in my assistant!" Laz steamed.

"Well, she's not really your assistant Laz" Dick corrected him "She's the VP of Sales… She may report to you, but she's not your assistant."

"Even so…" Laz protested.

"Plus" Dick continued "she told Doug she's the one who puts the report together each quarter… Says she has done for years!"

"Under my supervision!" protested Lazarus.

"Told him you hadn't actually picked up this quarter's presentation yet," Dick advised Lazarus with a nod, "I would watch that one if I were you Laz…"

Laz groaned as Aubrey informed them he had to go and 'do a thing'. "Dick," Aubrey asked, "call me when you're done here will you? I need to talk to you about something." Dick squirmed. Aubrey looked him in the eye, "Call me." Dick nodded.

"She's after your job Laz," Dick confided in Laz, "and you know Dangle has no time for you, me either really, and he likes a pretty face…'

"…and 36 double Ds" qualified Lazarus.

Dick and Aubrey were as much family to Laz as his own wife and flesh and blood. More, in fact, than Mary his wife who no longer seemed to be able to utter a civil word to him nor his children Stephen and Judith. Stephen only now having time for on-line video games played in his room behind a locked bedroom door, games he once played with his Dad when they were simpler and Laz still understood them, and Judith who reserved her love and time solely for her horses and came home most nights stinking of the barn.

Dick had always been a stalwart, but Laz was never sure whether he was a 'real friend' or just a colleague even though they went back many years. Certainly they spent a lot of time together outside of work as well as at the office, but they talked a lot of shop and Laz never felt like either had ever opened up to the other about their real feelings, their emotions.

On the surface, Aubrey was a great friend to have, a bit of an odd ball and a "Holy Roller" as Laz liked to call him sometimes. True Philadelphia society, he used to put it about that he was distantly related to Katharine Drexel, Philadelphia's very own saint, but these days he increasingly seemed to be absent from the club on the nights that Laz propped up the bar. The two of them had once been inseparable, but now Laz missed seeing Aubrey as much as he once did and wondered if he had a secret lover somewhere, man or woman? In spite of knowing him since college, Laz wasn't quite sure. Aubrey could easily be, thought Laz, "one of them…"

"How is the family?" asked Dick dutifully as they chomped through their steaks an hour or so, and several more scotches, later.

"Same old" sighed Laz "Mary barely talks to me any more. She's just happy enough doing her hunt dinners and non-stop charity events. She just rolls me out when the occasion suits."

"Ever thought of spending more time at home?" Dick suggested.

Laz's head jerked half upright and he answered immediately as he continued to chew "Are you kidding me? One of us would be dead by the end of the evening! Either me or Mary, or one of the kids! Anyway, Mary thinks I'm down here 'doing the deals,' 'spinning the wheels of commerce.'"

"And she's thought that for the last twenty years?" asked Dick doubtfully.

"Apparently so" confirmed Laz. The two men continued with their meal, the pleasant buzz that Laz had achieved a few hours ago had now turned to the beginnings of a thick muzziness that Laz knew was fueled as much by him screwing up tonight as by the drink. Not that this was the first time, there was a pattern and this seemed to be happening more and more often. First little things like missed appointments or phone calls with salesmen, then bigger things like losing his temper with his team, getting in late, making excuses to leave early, finding he was planning trips away from the office just to be away from the office. Doug Dangle glared at him every time he saw him now. Laz knew things were going South, but didn't know how to stop the spiral. Except by coming to the club.

"And anyway buddy" said Laz defensively to Dick, but mostly to himself "I've done pretty well for myself... I've got the house on the Main Line, I got the cars, I got the kids in private schools, I've got the shore house...'

"You sold the shore house Laz" Dick reminded him.

"What?" said Laz ordering two brandies.

"I said, you sold the shore house" repeated Dick.

"Oh yeah" said Laz "Well, what with Hurricane Sandy nearly moving it to Nantucket, what could I do?"

'And with your portfolio going through the toilet, not much else,' thought Dick.

The drinks came and Lazarus studied the brandy glass, slowly swirling the liquid round and round, cupping it and warming it in his hands. Then, almost religiously, taking a tiny sip, then suddenly a much bigger one. He stared deep into the amber. "Judith wants a new horse" he told the Cognac.

"I thought you just got her one?" Dick answered for the spirit.

"Rock star's girl's got a better one now" Laz answered the

liquid.

"How much this time?"

"Ten grand…" Laz lit up a cigar. This was about the only place in Philly you could smoke indoors now. Laz enjoyed that, Dick not so much.

Dick shook his head. They both sat in silence. The liquid remained the only thing in motion. "You have to say 'No' Laz…" someone or thing advised him through the fog and the smoke.

Laz looked up at Dick, his face was twisted in pain. "You have no idea do you?" he told him. "You're on your own, you have no idea what my life is like. If I say no, my life will be a living hell. Even the fucking dog will turn against me! Do you know how much havoc a sixteen year old girl can cause in a family? How much mayhem, how much misery?"

"What does Mary say?" asked Dick, who clearly had no idea.

"She says get the horse and let's hope like hell we have a peaceful Christmas for once…"

"And what about Stephen…" Dick asked about Laz's younger son.

Laz waggled his hands wildly together in front of himself, moving his fingers and thumbs crazily from one side to the other. "Happy as Larry as long as he's got one of those bloody computer games in his hands. Spends all night locked in his room playing it." Dick nodded "I'd be worried he was on drugs, but he never puts the controls down long enough to light anything up!"

The pair sat in silence for a few minutes. Lazarus contemplating his lot, Dick contemplating how to get Laz out of there without too much of a fuss.

"Laz" said Dick "You look pretty trashed Laz..." He waited for Lazarus to respond, but he just stared at his glass. "I just have to make a call and then I'll tell them to get you a cab. Remember, we have a budget meeting in the morning... Don't miss it" Dick wandered off towards the concierge desk, fumbling with his cell phone. He collected Laz's belongings and tipped the grateful coat check girl for him and, to the relief of many of the others dining in the Brandywine Room that night, he got Laz into his hat and coat.

Lazarus couldn't make it to the cab by himself so Dick and a doorman poured him into it. They gave the driver the address and a twenty and sent him on his way. The cold night air freshened Laz up a bit and, by the time he arrived home, he really thought he could get away with saying he'd only had one or two. The house was dark save for the flickering signs of game play coming from Stephen's room. That would go on for some hours still and in the morning the boy would complain he was too tired or too sick to go to school that day. What could you do?

He let himself in the back door and, as always, he was enthusiastically greeted by Dover the black lab. At least someone was always pleased to see him home he thought, well, most of the time. Dover scratched at the backdoor and Lazarus let him out into the garden for fear a tirade of whining and barking would wake up the house. He wandered past the liquor cabinet.

"I can probably get away with one more" he told himself, so he poured out three fingers of Scotch and nursed it in the chair by the dying fire. He dozed for a while, dropped the empty glass and awoke with a start. The glass was fine. He hid it behind the chair cushion and promised himself he would remember to find it in the morning. He stumbled upstairs and feeling his way along the walls to his bedroom, managed to approximate a state of undress and climb into bed.

He was out for the count within seconds, snoring heavily a few moments later. Sleep arrived quickly and soon he was dreaming he back in his younger, less complicated days before "all this". The dreams were short-lived, however, as suddenly he was awakened by a swiftly delivered elbow into the small of his back.

"Can't you not hear that?" his wife shouted at him. "Can you not hear the barking?" Then getting a good scent of her husband for the first time she added "God, you stink!"

He groaned "here we go again," as reality slowly reassembled itself for him, albeit in a vague, shapeless form.

"You left the fucking dog outside again you fool! She's waking up the entire neighborhood!" Mary screamed "It's twenty degrees out there. Go down and let her in!"

Laz could try and argue, but it wouldn't help, so he felt his way to the stairs and put his foot where the stair should have been. Almost, it seemed to him in slow motion, he fell through the air, crashing into the grand curving banisters, banging his neck and then rump on the hard marble steps as he rolled over and over. But, in what was really just a few seconds, he fell from the top step and crashed rapidly downwards to the bottom and was soon laying prone on the cold stone hallway floor, his limbs disagreeably twisted, with blood seeping from his head, mouth, nose and ears.

Lazarus Finds was dead.

THE FUNERAL

"SO THEY HAD to draw one of those ghastly chalk outlines on that lovely slate floor of your's?" Lazarus's sister Rebekah sympathized with Mary at the doors of St Peter's, Lower Wayne. She was a bitch, thought Mary, and she always did know just the right thing to say to push her buttons. "I hope Juanita will be able to get it out."

"No." Mary agreed, looking suitably mournful. "It is rather shocking to see that, right at the foot of the stairs. And too sad for the children to bear." She looked deep into the church where, up in the front row, the same pew where, in fact, her mother and father had sat on her wedding day, her two children now awaited the commencement of their father's funeral. Her daughter on the phone, seemingly agitated about something or other, probably crying on a friend's shoulder thought Mary. Her son, hunched head down, unable to look up or around, motionless except for the occasional bobbing of his head. "Poor children" she thought.

Her thoughts drifted back to the congregation of police in her front reception area that night, all gathered around Lazarus's prostrate body. The paramedics checked his vital signs but it was clear there was nothing they could do. Plus the smell of the booze mixed with the blood and, well there was no denying it, her husband had fouled himself somewhere between the seventh and bottom step and it all made for quite an unpleasant scene. They got through their work as professionally, and with as few questions for her, as possible. Mary knew Sergeant Frey from her work with Philly's Fallen Officers charities and he took her into the kitchen and made her a cup of tea.

"Was it usual for him to come home in this..." the officer hesitated "condition, Mrs Finds?" He paused. "I have to ask..."

Mary waved away his concern and took a sip of her tea, "No, of course, I understand..." she sighed "It's no secret Sergeant, Lazarus had a long standing, shall we call it, relationship with the bottle I'm afraid..."

"I have to say" the officer grimaced "judging by his, I guess, aroma he probably was in no condition to drive Mrs Finds..."

Mary looked shocked. "Oh Officer, Lazarus was very responsible - at least since his last DUI - he would have gotten a cab home... In fact, I think I heard it. A little after eleven, I think?"

"And the accident happened at 12:35am," deduced the officer emphasising the word accident, "so he would have been asleep an hour an a half?"

"Er, no." Mary shook her head. "He'd just come to bed. You'll probably find a glass behind the cushion in the chair by the fireplace. That's where he usually leaves it. " The officer seemed impressed by the woman's deduction. "Juanita goes straight to it each morning when she's loading the dishwasher," she advised him. "It's always there."

The stench on her late husband's breath, which a toxicity screen later showed him five times over the driving limit, the fact that he was still wearing his dress shirt, no underwear and just one sock, painted a fairly clear picture to Sergeant Frye who told Mary there would probably be no autopsy and she could go ahead with the funeral arrangements. Fortunately, she resisted confessing to the policeman that she had often wanted to push her husband down that very same staircase and that it was just good luck and timing that circumstance had taken its course before she had finally succumbed to that recurring desire.

"Mrs Finds… Mrs Finds…" it was the voice of the priest bringing her back to reality. Father Pratt paced backwards and forwards in the vestibule, looking at his watch, tapping it, then looking outside, up and down Montgomery Avenue. "We really should get on, it's passed eleven o'clock already…"

"They'll be here soon, Father," Mary called over to him "It's a terrible drive out from Center City at this time of day…"

"Mother couldn't make it…" Rebekah explained "…the cold." Mary nodded. "She felt it was bad enough losing one of the family just before Christmas rather than a brace of them"

Mary nodded understandingly. "Yes, I do know it takes quite the special event to get your Mother out of Sunny Acres these days. What was it last time?" Mary pondered, "the Ridley Hunt Ball wasn't it? Heaven forbid she should come to her own son's funeral!"

"It's freezing out, Mary dear!" Rebekah implored, as Father Platt continued to pace "and she couldn't understand why you didn't have a nice warm viewing at the funeral home."

"Because Rebekah," hissed Mary "because his body was so bent and black and blue, they could barely straighten it out enough to get it into the fucking coffin!" The expletive finally caused Father Platt to lose his patience and insist they finally get this show on the road.

For someone who had hundreds, perhaps thousands, of clients, twenty year's worth of associates from work and from the club and had lived in the Lower Wayne region all of his life, the attendance at the funeral was sparse to say the least. Of course, Mary had hurried things along as Judith was riding in the Winter Show on the following Saturday, the last gymkhana of the year, and delaying the funeral really would have played havoc with her eventing.

Since there was to be no viewing, Mary had declined to have Lazarus embalmed. It was her decision alone. Lazarus had always assumed he would be on the rare occasions when they had discussed such matters, but when Mary had heard that the embalming would add an extra thousand dollars or so to the final cost of the funeral and since no one would ever witness its effect, it seemed wasteful and silly. Plus, he was being cremated, so why embalm him just for a day or two, she had thought.

Mary also managed to save a bit on the coffin, her logic

again impeccable. Inside the beautiful white oak casket standing in front of the altar was another coffin made of thick blue cardboard that would become her late husband's final vehicle to eternity. The highly polished oak casket with the sparkling brass fittings was on the clock and had to be returned to the funeral home by five that evening.

It wasn't that Mary was concerned about her finances now that Lazarus had passed on, quite the opposite, since one of the most beneficial things about Lazarus working for Yours Mutual was that he was heavily insured. The company had always felt that their senior executives should be the epitome of the well protected man, set an example to their clients, and so gave them each a $10 million life insurance million policy. With double indemnity for the accident, Mary's bank account would soon swell by over twenty million dollars and Yours Mutual had promised to make the payment within days.

Mrs Finds had already found it hard to stop herself from letting slip, to the few of her friends she had seen since the accident, exact and minute details of the coming settlement and felt a deep and heart-warming joy as their eyes widened and jaws dropped in shock and envy. It was if she was flashing a new four carat diamond on her finger. Mary, however, was already dreaming about a little place in the Caribbean, St Bart's perhaps? Laz had never taken her anywhere nice that wasn't a sales force meeting or convention and she intended to change all that.

At the priest's direction, she made her way reluctantly to her seat beside the children. The congregation was sparse to say the least. In all there were only fifteen people at the service, thirteen if one didn't count the minister and organist, and the majority of the rest she didn't recognize. There didn't appear to be anyone at all from the company, not even Dick. She thought at least the board might attend, or at least a secretary or two, but perhaps the circumstances left them a little embarrassed. She had called them immediately, well she had to what with the insurance policy and everything, but instead of people they seemed to have sent rather a lot of flowers instead. Likewise the club had been informed, but no one here looked remotely like any member she'd seen on any of the few occasions she'd been allowed within those four walls.

Judith's dulcet tones reached her from three pews away. "Just have the fucking box there at 5am, OK?" she hissed down her phone, "I'm going to have to be there from three braiding her mane and getting her ready and I don't intend to be standing around in the cold any longer than I have to be!" Perhaps she hadn't been crying on a shoulder after all, thought Mary, though Stephen's head was still bobbing and his shoulders still heaving as she squeezed between the casket and the bench and into the pew.

"Stephen, do put away the Angry Birds" she implored. "There's a good boy" as the child wrestled with the game on his iPhone contorting his whole body as he did so.

"But Mom, please" the boy begged "I've nearly done level seventeen, it's taken the last half hour…" His thumb did a quick slide, tap, tap and he recommenced the level one more time.

"Judith… phone!" Mary ordered as sternly as she could.

"Mother! Horse!" Judith retorted as sternly, without having to act at all. "Can you spell H-O-R-S-E?" she sneered.

Mary sighed. "Then keep it down dear" she asked. "Put your head down and make it look like you're upset!"

Mary looked up. Father Pratt was ready to go. She managed a weak smile and nodded. St Bart's, she thought, or maybe St. Kitt's...

Father Platt nodded to the organist and she intoned the first few notes of "All Hail to Thee" as the priest motioned for the handful of the attendees to rise. This seemed to serve as a signal for three of the older ladies to make their way to the back of the church for a bit of a chat, lest the funeral interfere with what was clearly a regular social gathering for them. Mary and Rebakah mumbled their way through the hymn, the first of the selection that Mary had allowed the priest to make, as she and Laz had never been much of regular church goers and the only ones Laz really liked were Christmas carols which, although almost in season, hardly seemed appropriate the minister had had to remind her. At the end of just two verses, when it was apparent he was now singing on his own and, in fact, competing only with Judith's continued hissing down her cellphone at some blacksmith, the priest motioned them to sit.

"Dearly beloved" he began "we are gathered here today to celebrate the life, the all too short life, of a man - a good man," the priest qualified "a kind and giving husband and a loving father..."

"Yes!" cried Stephen from the front row, which warmed the priest's heart greatly but in reality merely indicated the boy had finally just managed to complete level seventeen.

"A man" continued Father Pratt, "who throughout his own career sought to bring security and hope to families, just like his own, to aid them through these most difficult and troubling times, and whose care and concern has no doubt helped hundreds if not thousands of wives and mothers like Mary, children like Judith and Stephen..."

Mary cast her eyes around the church as the priest droned on, hoping the contingent from Yours Mutual would arrive soon, but it didn't really matter. The claims adjuster had already been around to the house, all the paperwork was done, everything was just a formality now.

She saw the man from the local Firestone shop had arrived and seemed very upset. Not surprised, thought Mary, Laz always insisted on taking the Merc and the Audi there rather than the dealerships, just to save a few bucks. No wonder he was crying, no more two thousand dollar tune-ups for you Mr Patel, she thought. A few rows away were a couple of people who seemed to have come in off the street to get warm. Another couple of old ladies just appeared to enjoy a good funeral. A young black girl, about twenty, was either there to defrost or praying for something else or someone else, or looking to steal something. She too shed a tear now and then, though it seemed to bear no connection to what the minister was saying. Eventually, and to her relief, she heard the priest intone "All rise" and with some relief, Mary did.

"Dearly beloved" the priest concluded "since there will not be a service at the crematorium, anyone who would like to say a personal goodbye to Lazarus should make their way forward, once the family has concluded, and say a few final words." He blessed the casket with holy water, genuflected and, after placing one hand on each of Mary, Judith's and Stephen's shoulders, made his way to the back of the church.

Mary tapped the coffin gently. "Somehow Laz," she whispered, "I'm not at all surprised it ended this way." Rebekah too touched the coffin and took Mary's arm and walked her towards the main door. Judith dialed the number of the Radnor Saddlery and Stephen took another crack at level twenty one.

At the door, Rebekah steered Mary slightly to one side. "Mary dear," she half whispered "Mother wanted me to ask you a question."

"Oh yes" replied the grieving widow "what would that be?"

"Well," the sister-in-law responded nervously, "I know this isn't really the best time, but since you're not going back to the house or anything, well… there may not be another opportunity."

"Go on," replied Mary a little bit testily.

"Well, Mother was wondering, if there would be a will…" the sister-in-law stumbled. "A reading of Lazarus's will? Whether she, um, we should come?"

"Let me see," replied Mary "the mother of my husband, who decided she couldn't come to his funeral lest she might catch a cold and die of pneumonia, would now like to know when the reading of his will is, in case her son, thirty eight years her junior, might have left her some kind of inheritance?"

Rebekah squirmed, "Well you know Mother…"

"And you had the same thought?" queried Mary.

"Well, maybe even a memento?" suggested the sister-in-law.

"Well, let me think… " responded the wide-eyed-widow searching her memory. "As I recall, Laz left behind the house, the cars, portfolio, the savings… Oh and the death in service benefit, plus the twenty million dollar insurance policy."

Rebekah's mouth fell open.

"And the last time we met the lawyers and re-did the wills he insisted your mother and you were both named in them!" Mary explained.

"He did?" exclaimed Rebekah, all excited now.

"And he left you both the same thing" Mary confirmed.

"How much" asked Rebekah "He was always so good to us."

Mary smiled "He left you both… one dollar."

Rebekah looked like she had been shot "One dollar" she shouted "he left us one dollar?"

"Yes!" Mary confirmed, "He didn't want you to think you'd been left out by accident! I do so wish I could be there when you tell your mother, but I have things to do." The widow made to set off, but thoughtfully added, "Do make sure you have your mother's nitro standing by…"

And with that, Mary gathered up Judith and Stephen and left Rebekah alone with her brother at St Peter's Church, Lower Wayne.

THE CREMATORIUM

THE FRANKLIN FIELDS Cemetery was one of the cities oldest and, although areas of it had fallen into disrepair and had been taken back by the adjoining woods of Fairmount Park, it was believed that the graveyard held the remains of Civil War soldiers, though no one was quite sure of their location any more. In 1992, after much controversy, the City had permitted the tearing down of the old gatehouse and the building of a new funeral chapel and, the first of its kind in the city, a crematorium.

Jonas Reinfeldt had been the superintendent and operator of the crematorium since its very first day. A time when it was considered to be a state-of-the-art facility and had attracted professional visitors from all around the country, visitors who came to admire the brand new, polished and gleaming furnace imported all the way from Jonas's native Sweden. Jonas had arrived with the furnace to hire and train local operators and, finding all the candidates eminently unsuitable to be trusted with this fine piece of machinery, Jonas had never left. He had looked after the R-32 until this very day and had seen nearly fifty thousand corpses pass through its portal and was determined to pass that milestone within the next three years, before his mandatory retirement forced him to hand the keys onto a younger man.

"Or woman!" he chuckled to the sixteen-year-old Laura Delaney who was spending a weeks work experience with him, "who knows? It could be you! Would you like that?" Jonas continued dusting and polishing. He was always cleaning and shining. Considering what went on here, it was as spotless and germ-free as any operating theatre one could ever hope to be taken into.

"I would so love that" exclaimed the girl "that would be SO cool!" her eyes glinting.

Jonas had had a lot of interns, co-op and work experience students spend time with him over the last ten years or so, apparently the stock market crash and economic downturn had made many young people realize that there really only was one industry that was truly recession proof, but none of his students had ever shared the same level of enthusiasm and passion for his work as did Laura.

He patted the furnace lovingly on its side as he checked the temperature. "Now, what are we looking for?"

"Optimum operating temperature between 1,500 and 2,000 degrees Fahrenheit…" answered the girl.

"But…" cued the man.

"But the R-32 gauges are in Celsius, so it should be between 816 and 1,094 C" she advised him.

"Very good" said Jonas tapping the gauge which read just 413 C "I like to go for a nice…"

"Even 900 C," finished Laura. "That way it doesn't stress the furnace too much, but it's still plenty hot enough to do the job."

Jonas smiled. He was old school. He never thought he'd be in favor of women entering the industry and when they told him a teenaged girl wanted to do work experience, he was dead set against it. But they'd been right, this one was just like he himself had been at that age.

"Do you think they'll ever replace the R-32?" asked the girl. Jonas looked shocked. "You know" she continued "with something faster…"

"Faster?" he asked "You can't burn a body faster! It still takes…"

"I know, one hour per hundred pounds body weight…" she sighed "but the R-32 is so slow to pre-heat."

Jonas polished the brass wheel that opened the door to the furnace cavity, "I don't know what's wrong with you kids today. Always in a hurry you are…" though he knew what she meant and felt the R-32, rather like him, was probably on the way out. The door bell rang. "Get that Laura" he added sadly "Could be the first one of the day. 'Mr Lazarus Finds'."

Laura made her way to a double door at the side of the building and opened it. A wintery chill blew in. Two men in dark suits stood there, behind them a hearse had been backed up against the door, engine still running.

"Mr Lazarus Finds?" Laura asked cheerfully.

The men looked taken aback by the pretty schoolgirl greeting them, but were brought back to reality by Jonas's scream from within. "Switch your Javia engine off! Are you trying to kill us all in here? One of us is dead already for Javia's sake." Laura had looked up 'Javia' on her first day, she knew what it meant now even if the undertakers didn't. She was using it at home already. 'I don't have any Javia homework…, Mind your own Javia business…' 'Javia' was a useful word to know.

"Bring Mr Finds in please" instructed Laura. Engine switched off, the two men unloaded the coffin onto the charger and wheeled it inside. Jonas pointed to a table, one of several used for queuing the clientele. Can you place the casket on table number one please?

Sorry Jonas" said one of the men "it's a rental…"

Jonas cast his eyes to heaven "Min Gud" he said "another rental… Can nobody afford a casket these days?"

More bad news for you Jonas" said the other "not embalmed either I'm afraid." The two men took the top off the beautiful polished oak casket and lifted out the thick blue cardboard coffin that lay hidden within.

"Gud I Himlin" Jonas shook his head "so poor they cannot even afford to embalm the poor soul…"

"Poor?" laughed one of the men "Rich bitch if you like!" Jonas tutted at the man's use of language.

"Main Line sort" said the other.

Jonas made a face towards Laura then looked back towards the two men "Is he, um," he asked "leaking at all?"

The men took a look around the base of the box. "Nothing obvious" said one. "But then he only died on Monday night" said the other "and it's only, what, Thursday now?"

"Could save him for tomorrow if you wanted" laughed the other.

"Out, komma ut" shouted Jonas at them, "and take your cheap rental coffin with you. We will take care of Mr Finds and give him the dignity that you and his family deemed not to show him!" And with that the undertakers rolled their charger away leaving Jonas and Laura with their first customer of the day.

"Some music, I think" said Jonas to Laura and Lazarus. "If I were leaving this world today, this is what I would want to listen to…" The man shuffled through a small collection of CDs next to a small compact disc player on the shelf and selected Sibelius's Violin Concerto in D Minor. "He would like this, I think…"

"Now Laura…" he advised "let's go through the check list."

"OK" said Laura enthusiastically pulling out a notepad and pen from her bag. "I'm ready…"

Over the next twenty minutes Jonas and Laura checked the documents from the undertaker and the paperwork from the coroner and hospital; his client was a fairly young man, early fifties, no pacemaker to worry about;

"Why Laura?"

"Because they can cause an explosion in the corpse?"

"And..." added Jonas.

"And possibly damage the R-32?" she concluded as Jonas nodded, reassured.

"No brass fittings to remove..." Laura looked sadly at Jonas.

"Afraid not..." Jonas sighed, knowing Laura liked doing this job and it had been her responsibility to do so all week. There's another one this afternoon though..." he added cheerfully.

They checked the record number on the cremation permit to the markings on the box. They matched, they were good to go.

"It is so, so important to make sure the remains get back to the right family." Jonas stressed to the girl "and I would feel terrible if I ever had made a mistake and sent back the incorrect ashes to the loved ones. What a dreadful thing that would be!" he scolded Laura, though, unknowingly, he had already done just that done that twelve or so times already in his thirty years at Franklin Fields - even though it was rather hard for anyone to know or ever find out, and the remains had received just the same dignified love and respect they would have deserved had they ended up in their planned location. More, in some cases.

Jonas kept glancing at his watch. He had a service coming in at noon, followed by another immediate cremation. R-32 was still only hovering just above 800 C and the family for the 12 o'clock had started to arrive already. He should have switched on earlier, but he had been telling Laura stories of his early days growing up in the funeral home in Malmo, where the ground was so frozen from November until April that no one got buried and everyone would be kept in a barn out back of the undertakers. Then come May, there would be funerals from sunrise to sunset. The girl had been so fascinated that Jonas had gotten carried away in telling the stories and fallen far behind in his day despite an early start.

The congregation looked like they would easily pack out the chapel for the noon service. Jonas never got involved with them. He was the mechanic of death as far as they were concerned, but he could see into the chapel through a small one-way window and the family and friends of this person soon filled it to bursting. He and Laura peeked through and she decided this would be a good time for lunch. He turned off the concerto and listened as the organist struck up the first few notes of "My God, my God – All Hail to Thee" - not one of his personal favorites.

R-32 was almost up to temperature and while they could have got a start on Mr Finds, Jonas didn't like to incinerate one customer while another was outside waiting for delivery. He felt it too disturbing to the relatives. To see your own loved one's smoke was acceptable, to realize they

were in a queue for the process and someone else was
already getting burned, made it feel too much of a
production line. They took out the Wawa sandwiches that
Laura had picked up on the way in that morning and sat
down and waited. Jonas regaled her with more stories of
the summer funeral rush and she was amazed by how much
money he could make in tips from relatives who had long
gotten over their grief and now wanted their relatives
interred as expeditiously as possible. She pondered a
career in Sweden over her Italian and Cheese sub.

They had finished their foot-longs and smoothies just as the
chapel conveyor started up. Automatically, the curtains
parted and their second client of the day arrived to wait her
turn to the strains of "Rock of Ages" filtering through from
the organ.

"Let's wait a few minutes, Laura" Jonas advised. "We'll
wait just a little while before we sent Mr Finds through."

Laura nodded "Shall I get to work on the hardware on this
one then Jonas?" she asked, with a bit of a glint in her eye.

He smiled, "Yes, why don't you do that. No one likes large
lumps of melted brass delivered in your loved one's ashes,
plus it's very bad for the R-32" he reminded her.

Jonas peeked through the one-way window. The chapel
was nearly empty. A few guests lingered looking at the
array of flowers and wreaths that had been left in the
receiving area and then slowly they drifted off too. The
furnace was at 895 C perfect for a fast burn with a
cardboard coffin. Mr Finds should be done within an hour

and a half or so. Jonas maneuvered the blue box up onto the sliding ramp into the incinerator. With a final friendly tap on the top of the makeshift casket, a custom Jonas had practiced on nearly fifty thousand coffins over the years, the technician readied to depress the button that would start the sequence that would send Lazarus back to the ashes from whence he had come.

From behind him he heard a low groan. "What did you say Laura?" he asked.

Laura stopped unscrewing a handle. "Nothing" she answered.

Then again Jonas heard a groan and a soft shuffle or shift. He listened carefully and then from within the cardboard coffin he heard a voice clearly say "Jesus Christ… This is the worst fucking hangover I have ever had…"

Behind him he heard the sound of brass falling and then Laura whispered "Crazy…"

Jonas put his arm protectively around the girl and looked back at the box "Mind your language Sir" was all he could say "I've got a javia child out here!"

THE HOSPITAL

LAZARUS LAY UNCONSCIOUS in the hospital bed in the Intensive Care Unit. His limbs laid outstretched before him, rigid in their fiberglass bandages and suspended in mid-air. His head immobilized on the pillow with a frame of steel rods prohibiting even the slightest motion. Tubes entered each nostril and wrist and crept under the sheets to his nether regions. An air and oxygen mix was pumped though his mouth via a respirator which, for now, did his breathing for him.

Mary stood at the foot of the bed. She stared at the mass of tubes and casts and bandages in front of her, scarcely able to believe what had taken place these last twenty-four hours. The doctor had given her some valium and, sometimes, she felt that she had dreamed the whole thing but, looking at this mess of a human being in front of her, she knew this was very, very real.

"You know Laz" she told him, though she knew he was far too sedated to hear her, "when they told me, and they said 'You'd better sit down dear… You're not going to believe this…' when they told me… I didn't doubt them for a second…"

She moved over and sat in a dark green and equally deeply uncomfortable vinyl chair at the side of the bed.

"I didn't doubt them at all Laz… When they said, 'You

won't believe this Mary, Lazarus is alive, he has survived…'" She stared at her husband as his chest slowly raised and lowered itself in timing to the mechanical beat of the respirator.

"When they expected me to faint or to start crying hysterically, I just sat there and thought to myself 'that son-of-a-bitch has gone and done it to me again'"

Mary wiped a tear from her eye. To anyone viewing through the window from the corridor they were witnessing a scene of deep love and affection, of care and concern, of hope and prayer not one of hate and long lasting, deep seated resentment.

"Only this was the cruelest joke yet Laz" she continued "we'd gotten used to you making promises to us and breaking them over the years, me, the children even Dover. But this was one I thought you had actually gone through with. But no, you had to wake up…" Mary's voice got louder. "You had to fucking wake up!"

"He will" said a soothing voice from someone beyond the bed and the beeping life support systems.

Mary swiveled around to see a middled aged nurse had walked in and started checking Laz's vital signs. "What?" said Mary.

"He will wake up" said the nurse taking her notes "in time… But don't go getting yourself all upset. We don't want you getting yourself any more upset than you are, do we?"

Mary viewed her suspiciously, but did she really care what she had heard? "I'm supposed to be seeing the consultant," she said. "Will he be along soon, do you know? I've been here forever..."

"It's a she," corrected the nurse and looking at her watch. "Dr Moriarity. She should be along in five minutes or so. She said she'd be down at seven." The nurse smiled at Mary. "Can I get you a cup of tea?" she offered. Mary shook her head, she would wait without tea.

At a few minutes after seven o'clock on the evening of the day of the funeral of Lazarus Finds, the door opened to his ICU room and Dr. Sandi Moriarity wandered in. Mary thought she looked like a scatterbox from the moment she saw her. She had all the accoutrements of a doctor, a white coat, stethoscope, pager and such but she was as thin as a bird with crazy, wild red hair, wearing a mask and latex gloves as if she had just come from the theater. In her hand she held Laz's chart which she had grabbed from the door on the way in.

"So, how's the resurrected Mr Finds?" she asked.

Mary jumped out of her chair and headed towards her. "Are you..."

"Sandi Moriarity" said the consultant "No hand shaking! I won't touch you. Too many infections in hospitals!" She held her hands back as if in an act of surrender. "Did you know the CDC, that the Center of Disease Control reckon there are 1.7 million people get sick in hospitals every year who were fine when they went in there?"

"Um, no" answered Mary.

"Well, in fact" the consultant went on, "it's probably several times higher than that. So just stay over there" she said pointing to the chair "and I'll stand over here."

"What about him?" said Mary pointing to Lazarus.

"And say away from him too, if you don't mind" the doctor told her. "I just put him back together again."

"Can I just ask how my husband is doing?" hissed Mary.

"Well, he's lucky to be alive!" answered the consultant.

"Are the injuries that serious?' Mary leaned forward and added, almost hopefully, "life threatening?"

"No, I mean, he's lucky to be alive!" explained the doctor. "They nearly incinerated him!"

"But how's his health?" Mary almost shouted.

The doctor bristled. She didn't like this one. He might have been better off not making it, she thought. She looked at the notes, tapped them a couple of times, nodded once or twice, turned some pages, made a mental note to stop at Whole Foods on the way home and pick up some bread, eggs and milk or, if she had time, Wegmans.

"Pain de Campange" she eventually said, realizing too late

she was finishing her shopping list aloud. "Severe Head Trauma!" the surgeon covered quickly hoping this woman didn't understand French or shop at Wegmans. "Your husband has a severe head trauma, which caused the prolonged lack of consciousness. Plus the broken legs and broken arm, all laying unset for nearly three days, have not contributed to his overall well-being at all."

Mary sighed "I probably could have guessed that much by looking at him, Doctor"

Mary shook her head "I don't understand how this could have happened. He was three seconds from being burned alive! What kind of hospital is this?"

"Mrs Finds, the intern who signed your husband's death certificate has been put on administrative leave," Moriarity advised her. "He feels terrible, but the extremely low blood pressure your husband must have had could have led any doctor to believe he was dead."

"But surely he was thoroughly checked?" insisted Mary.

Dr Moriarity looked from side-to-side, "between you and me Mrs Finds, from what I heard when they brought him in, your husband was so covered in shit and urine and blood and alcohol and vomit that four interns tossed a coin to see who was going to have to deal with him…"

"Is that any way to talk about a patient?" asked Mary.

"Well, let's just say" confessed the consultant "back in my intern days in Butte Montana, I'd probably just have poked him with a stick!"

"I am going to speak to my lawyers about this!" threatened Mary.

"Hey, Mrs Finds' Dr Moriarity snapped back, "are we hear to talk about your husband and his health or a lawsuit?"

Mary wasn't sure how to answer that, in her heart of heart's she'd rather talk about a lawsuit, but she knew her lawyers would be advising her to speak to them first anyway.

"Fine" she relented "let's talk about him"

"Let me put it this way" explained the consultant "It's still early, but it's promising.   It'll be a slow recovery, but he should regain some limited functionality within a few weeks. Then we can assess any long term effects."

"So long term... will he survive?" asked Mary, somewhat betraying her disappointment.

"He may have some brain trauma, but the scans look good. He had lost a lot of blood when they brought him back in here, but luckily the cardboard coffin helped form some sort of a bandage – he was quite stuck to it when we got to him. Honestly, I was scared they'd rip his head off when they were trying to get him out of there."

Mary's eyes widened "I am so going to sue this hospital!"

"Now, now, now Mrs Finds, he's in the best possible hands now. Now that he's on the fifth floor and not in the morgue anyway, and we can rebuild him... And I don't think it'll cost six million dollars!" She chuckled.

"No, it'll cost you a lot more that six million dollars by the time I'm through with you" said Mary.

The doctor paused and then continued a little bit haughtily "I'm not sure how the limbs will heal. They've been un-set for a while. He'll probably have weakness in both legs but we will get there." She gave Laz and Mary each a little wave. "See you on the ward" the doctor told them as she left.

Mary walked back to the foot of the bed and held onto the rails. She stared down at Laz. All her dreams had evaporated in just a few hours. Oh, she knew her friends were all mocking her now, joking about her place in St Barts or St. Kitts. She knew Rebekah and his mother were having a good old laugh right now.

She noticed Laz's limbs starting to sway gently and then more and more vigorously, from side-to-side. In spite of the steel frame around it, his head began to wobble backwards and forwards. At first Mary thought it might be an earthquake, but they were virtually unknown in this part of the world, and then she realized it was she who was shaking. It was her anger leaving her body in violent tremors and rocking Laz's bed from side to side. It felt good and it felt right. She would show them. She would have the last laugh after all. No one would stop her from getting what she truly deserved, not Lazarus, not Rebekah and his mother, not even her Main Line friends. She deserved more than this and, just for a few glorious seconds she had tasted it and it was delicious and she would not be denied!

The numerous pumps working to keep Laz alive started to sound erratic and the bags beneath the bed listed back and forth and the machines that were beeping steadily a few moments ago began to sound more and more agitated. Alarms started to go off as the shaking increased and Mary could not stop it and was unable to let go. It was as if she and the bed were now one.

"Twenty million dollars!" she cried. "Twenty million dollars... Just think what we could have done with that! And instead all I'm left with is a miserable, drunken, fucking cripple..."

Those were the first words Laz heard as he drifted back to consciousness and the nurses rushed to his assistance.

THE RECOVERY

LAZ RECOVERED SLOWLY.

Dr Moriarity thought that the story of his narrow escape should be withheld from him for as long as possible, for fear that it might shock him so much as to cause his already weak heart too much strain. Mary was in favor of him being told right away.

"Surely, as a public service" she insisted "he should be telling his story to the world. If only to ensure such a terrible event doesn't befall some other hapless victim?"

"Somehow, I can't imagine the universe quite aligning that exact same way for quite some time, " insisted the consultant, who was adamant even after Mary sold her story to People magazine and a posse of journalists and photographers showed up on the fifth floor.

"Get out of here" Moriarity had shouted at them, "or I'll be putting all of you in ICU and we'll see how you like that that!" The media had scattered ahead of the fiery haired and tempered doctor, fleeing down the emergency stairwell and never daring to come back, moving instead onto Lindsay Lohan's latest court appearance and Angelina's upcoming trip to Cambodia to buy a new baby.

Mary, after much persuasion and then the threat of legal action, was forced to return the $100,000 payment that she had negotiated for the exclusive. She unsuccessfully tried to convince the editors to hold the story until Lazarus was healthier, but by then CNN had already run with it and the magazine had lost interest.

"I'm adding the $100k on to the lawsuit," Mary assured Dr Moriarity.

"Six million one hundred thousand and counting…" Moriarity responded.

Lazarus didn't remember too much about his time in the hospital, which was probably just as well. The staff treated him well. They felt, frankly, sorry for him. He didn't have many visitors and most of the time he just stared up at the ceiling. For a while they thought he might have suffered some undiagnosed brain injury, but eventually Dr Moriarity decided he was just deeply depressed, and probably had been before the fall.

Christmas was a big blur. But Laz seemed to remember the decorations going up in the hallway and a nurse checking that he wasn't Jewish before putting a miniature tree on his side table. But he was still quite ill and sore then. He was still getting fevers and terrible headaches. He recalled Mary coming in one time about then. He had been trying to ask her what he was doing there, but he couldn't get the words out.

He pictured, from the movies, the scene where the sick or dying man was trying to say something, when everyone stopped, came nearer, listened intently and said, "I think he's saying… 'Tell Laura…, tell Laura…"

But with Mary it was the opposite. He remembered that day quite well. She was standing at the foot of the bed talking, and he couldn't really understand what she was saying, it was all being said so fast, and he really wanted to know why he was there, and what had happened to him. So he tried to speak, and it was hard Really, really hard. He hadn't used his lips and tongue and mouth much at all since the accident. So he licked his lips and tried to form some words, tried to push through some air to make them make a sound, tried to get his wife's attention, get her to come to his bedside.

"Murh…" he said.

Mary stopped talking for a second.

"Murhhhh…" he said again.

Mary rolled her eyes slightly "Very good Lazarus" she said "M-a-r-y…"

"Murh-ry…" Laz completed the work.

"Very good Laz," Mary smiled, "now do let me finish, dear, or I shall be terribly late… So, I have so much to do this week… I still have to do all the charity work for the club and the hunt, you know - collecting presents for orphaned and poor children, I'm decorating St. Agnes's for the upcoming midnight mass with the ladies, plus I'm attending end-of-year school concerts and plays…"

Laz was already exhausted and his brow was dripping with

perspiration from the exertion.

"Ma-rry.." He tried again.

"Yes Laz" she hurriedly confirmed. "So I'm not going to
be here much over the next week or so, up to Christmas
anyway and then of course there's the New Year's Eve
party at the Bellevue to get ready for." She looked down at
the mass of bandages in the bed below her. "So you'll have
to be a brave little soldier and get by, alright Laz?"

"Ma-ry…" said Laz with a final exhaustive effort.

"Very good Laz… Keep it up!" and with that she gave him
a wave and headed for the door, turned into the corridor
and made for the elevator.

"I hear he's talking" shouted Moriarity from the nurse's
station. "Thanks for telling us…"

He remembered Judith coming by after that. His speech
was getting better by then, still just single words and small
phrases, but at least he could communicate more, even if
the heavy medication made what he said somewhat non-
sensical sometimes.

It must have been the first time Judith had been there, he
realized, because she seemed quite taken aback, even
shocked. That much, at least, pleased Laz. The girl
observed the limbs in traction, the head immobilized by the
steel frame, the tubes into his nostrils, the bags hanging
under the bed, with other tubes snaking God knows where.

"What do they all do" she asked.

Laz tried his best to explain, "Wrist for meds, nose for food, drain in side, drip other wrist…"

"Ugh" Judith almost shriveled "how do you get up and go to the bathroom?"

Laz wondered how a girl who spent half her life around horses could know so little about bodily functions of the human kind. "Don't… catheter…" then realizing he girl didn't know what a catheter was explained 'tube, from my winky… to the bag…"

Judith nearly threw up. "God! That is so gross!" she almost shouted "TMI - already! Disgusting…"

Laz lay back looking at the girl going through mock vomit gestures. "Not gross" he explained "Should have got one years ago…"

Judith paced up and down at the end of the bed before addressing what had really fetched her to her father's bedside.

"So I suppose you heard I lost to Samantha?" she said at last.

Laz half smiled, now knowing why she was here at last. "No" he answered "no one said…"

"Well? What do you expect" Judith turned hands on hips "she's only got an ex-Olympic trials horse now that cost over $50,000!"

"Oh" said Laz, tiring.

"What chance have I got?" she asked, staring at her father.

'What chance have I got' thought her father, staring at the ceiling.

"I'll never be able to beat her, until I get a new horse…" Judith explained. "A better horse!" She glared down at Laz.

"She get better one then…" Laz tried to explain the obvious, knowing that the daughter of a millionaire, no a billionaire, rockstar was always going to be able to out-equine him any day.

"There's this Oldenburg for sale at Radnor." Judith ignored him, "they want $30,000 for him. But I can get him for twenty, I'm sure. He's beautiful. He nearly went to Beijing Daddy!" she pleaded.

For a moment Laz had an image of a horse on vacation in China, going down the Yangtze River, eating noodles with chopsticks, having its picture taken on the Great Wall, then realized his daughter meant the Olympics. He looked at the girl, her half-cocked head, her little smile, those bright blue eyes that always seemed to be able to get the better of him. It was like she was three years old again and they were down at Penn's Landing and she wanted another ice cream. Had he ever been able to resist that look?

"No…" he said, realizing it was a gift not being able to say many words.

"What" shouted Judith "What do you mean 'No'? I have to have him! And I need to tell them today, otherwise somebody else will get him. I've got to tell them 'Yes' today Daddy - so you'll just have to change your mind!"

Laz closed his eyes and took a deep breath, he pressed his morphine pump the maximum five times. "No" he repeated.

"Fuck you" said the girl "Mom was right, you are nothing but a pathetic loser…'

"Get out!" the voice came sharp and short from the door "Get out now!"

"Who are you?" asked Judith.

"I'm his freaking doctor sweetie" Moriarity told her "who the hell are you?"

Judith stood as tall and straight as she could. "I'm his daughter" she announced proudly.

Moriarity looked her up and down. "I don't think so" she told the girl "if he'd had a daughter, she'd had been in here long before now. Now get the hell out before I call security!"

Laz shut his eyes tight.

"Dad!" cried Judith.

"The patients asleep," explained Moriarity "now scram!"

Judith grabbed her bag and flounced out of the room and headed for the exit.

Moriarity looked over at Laz. "You OK, hon?" she asked. Laz didn't reply, but a tear formed and ran down his cheek. She took a tissue and wiped it away and left the room.

Laz knew Stephen visited fairly often, on his way back from school, more to avoid seeing his mother at home than anything else. Laz slept through most of the visits and Stephen would sit in the large green, vinyl lounger in the corner of the hospital room, headphones on, playing "Angry Birds" or "Tour of Duty". Moriarity would tell him to talk to his father, but he never did. He just sat there, transfixed to the screen, tapping and swiping, swiping and tapping. Still, it was nice for him to have someone in the room Moriarity thought.

Christmas came and went and Laz received no visitors nor gifts, though Mary did produce the Oldenburg for Judith as she'd wanted, not at the hospital of course. Santa brought Stephen a new X-box 360 and a $1,500 Game Stop gift card. Mary treated herself to an outfit from Eileen Fisher she'd had seen a month or so ago in the New York Times Magazine. Stephen suggested they all visit his Dad on Christmas Day but Mary felt 'peace and quiet' were the best gifts they could give him.

New Year's Eve passed pretty much the same way. Mary at

a bash at 19 in the Bellevue Hotel, wearing the new ensemble and receiving many "ooh's and ah's" and envious looks from across the restaurant, attention that made her feel a tiny bit better about not having the twenty million dollars or the place in St. Barts. But just a tiny bit. Aubrey from the club had invited her as his guest and it was lovely to sit at his table and be treated like a lady for a change. Judith at the barn for a sleepover where she got very sick doing Jaegermeister shots and ended up passed out on a mountain of hay bales, incurring a nasty straw rash on her face by morning which lasted until she went back to school. Stephen playing in a worldwide FIFA 2013 competition, eventually losing in extra time to some kid in The Gambia, wherever that was, neither noticed midnight come and go, nor the dawn arrive.

Just before midnight Moriarity came in with the patient's sleeping pill. "You still awake Laz?" she asked, knowing he was.

"Still awake" he confirmed.

"Mind if I park it?" she pointed to the green, vinyl lounger.

"Your chair" volunteered Laz.

"Nearly Midnight" said Moriarity, gesturing to the TV, "do you want to see the ball drop?"

"No" said Laz, who would have shook his head if he could, "having too much fun this year…"

Moriarity laughed "Yeah, I guess you are… This will sure

be one to remember" she confirmed, "or maybe forget?"

"We'll see" said Laz.

"Do you remember much about it yet?" asked the doctor.
"Or do you just remember what you've been told?"

Laz had been thinking long and hard over the holidays
about what had beset him and the circumstances that had
brought the accident about. The details came back in little
dribs and drabs. At one point he panicked thinking his Audi
may still be in that parking lot across from the club getting
charged $50 a day or ripped to pieces by thugs, but Mary
had thought of that and Dick had kindly recovered it the
day after the accident. He remembered being drunk, (not
much new there) but he couldn't remember how he got
home. He recalled getting up out of bed, was it to go to the
bathroom (as these were the pre-catheter days) or was it to
get Mary her interminable glass of water? Why didn't she
just take one to bed with her instead of waking him in the
middle of the night saying "I'm so thirsty… I should get
myself a glass of water," and then continue to lie there
while his catholic altar boy guilt gnawed at him until he
finally jumped out of bed to get it for her? "Oh, you don't
have to do that" she would say, but then she would smile
quietly to herself in the darkness. He could almost see it.

"Remember getting up" he said at last. "Had to go
downstairs"

"But you'd had a lot to drink" volunteered the Doctor.

Laz thought hard "Mary wanted water" he said at last.

Moriarity muttered "bitch" under her breath. "And then…"

"Flying…" said Laz. At the top of the stairs something had happened. Could it be that she pushed him? No, Mary would never do that, she was too settled in bed at night to get up even for that. But, he remembered launching into the air, like a hang glider or Superman even, then crashing and rolling and tumbling and then pain, lots of pain, before a gentle warmth came over him and he drifted back to sleep.

Moriarity heard the patient humming. 'It was Mahler' she thought 'Symphony No. 2 in C minor'

Laz remembered the music all around him. He was at ball in Imperial Russia and he was dancing with this incredibly beautiful woman. And the orchestra was playing the music from that cat food commercial. He remembered feeling wonderful, dancing round and round with everything and everyone in the grand ballroom all revolving around them.

"And did you feel pain" asked Moriarity.

Laz stopped humming and the orchestra stopped playing and he felt like he'd suddenly lost something.

"No, no pain" he said "just felt happy…"

The doctor stared down at the broken man that she had tried to piece back together, picked up the remote control and said "Come on you! We're going to watch that ball drop! Next year, is going to be a way better year for you!"

THE REHAB

LAZ'S FRACTURED SKULL mended nicely, the arm was the least of his worries, his legs, having been broken and then re-broken took the longest time to heal and by February he was still unable to get around on crutches. However, the hospital's job was done and Moriarity had made him as healthy as she could. The porter helped Laz into a wheelchair and the consultant tucked a blanket around him.

"Are you sure you wouldn't rather be going home, Laz?" she asked him.

"No, I'll be fine" he assured her. "Mary's worried about the stairs and all…"

"Well, surely you could sleep on the ground floor?" she asked, picking up the few possessions he had and packing them into a plastic bag.

"I could," agreed Laz. "But Mary's having cleaners in to get the stains out of the slate in the hallway. She fired Juanita because she couldn't get it out before the Christmas party. It seems the new maid is having no better luck."

"But you could still get driven in every day for rehab?" assured the doctor.

Laz shook his head. "You have no idea of Mary's schedule

do you? She certainly couldn't do it. I haven't seen my friends since the accident. Judith only knows how to get to the barn and back" He look back over his shoulder at the doctor, "Trust me, I'm better off as an in-patient at the rehab center. At least they'll be able to get my dammed legs moving properly again!"

She touched him on the shoulder, "Well come back and see me, you miserable bastard. Not many of my patients ever survive, so it's nice to see one once in a while!" The porter started to wheel him away, but Laz stopped him and made him turn him around.

"Thanks Sandi" he said "not just for this" gesturing to himself, "but for everything," and with his good arm he extended a finger and tapped it to the side of his head.

"Ah, get out of here you pussy, before I break the other one," she cried, but she nodded too.

The rehabilitation center in Paoli was further away from home that the hospital, but had a reputation that was second to none on the East coast. They put Laz on an intensive program of physical therapy and counseling that, though rigorous, soon had him moving his legs and left arm again, albeit painfully. He actually relished the hard work every day and didn't mind the excuse Mary made that the extra five mile drive made it almost impossible for her to visit him more than once a week.

Laz got used to his solitude. He used his time alone to think over his life, especially since college, of the roller coaster he had been on since getting married, since joining

Yours Mutual. How just getting through each day had become his day's ambition. How he had wasted the last twenty or more years. He thought a lot about it, he didn't know what to do about it, but he knew that change had to come. He just couldn't see what that change would look like.

Eventually Dick showed up in his room late one night. He smelled of whiskey, reminding Laz that it must be a couple or even three months since he last had a drink. He felt OK about that. His liver was probably over the moon and he wondered if he could keep it up once he was off the Perocet and out in the world again. Did he need the whiskey, or did he just need the club to escape the world, his world?

Dick poked his head around the corner of his door. "How are you doing?" he asked.

"Not too bad, considering I've got a fractured skull, broken arm and two mangled legs. How's the club? How's Aubrey?"

"Fine, someone else buying his drinks for him now"

"Where the hell have you been?" asked Laz.

Dick looked contrite.

"I'm sorry. It's just these last few months have been ridiculous at the office, especially with you not being there…"

"I'm here weekends too, you know" advised Laz.

"Yes, I know" said Dick "It's just that once I didn't come for a while, then… well, I was too embarrassed to come. I thought I had left it too long"

"What about Aubrey?" asked Laz.

"Oh, yeah… he told me to tell you he came a few times, but you were asleep" Dick advised.

"Lying bastard" said Laz.

Dick laughed "You'll never get him to admit it, you know."

"You're looking well…" Dick told him.

Laz supposed, apart from the injuries which were now no longer obvious, he was in some of the best shape of his life, even if his ambulatory skills were pretty poor. "Healthy eating and no booze for three months will do that, I guess" replied Laz.

"Mind if I sit" Dick asked motioning to the edge of the bed.

Laz shrugged. "Just don't breathe on me" he asked.

He sat. "I've missed you, you know…"

"There's Aubrey…" Laz advised.

"He's hardly ever there Laz," Dick told him, "plus it was Christmas. It just wasn't the same. No one to bitch and complain about work with!"

"You know, I hardly ever think about it," Laz confessed, "and they've been awfully good not hassling me."

Dick cleared his throat, the smell of whiskey filled the room. "I'm sure Clarence will be in touch" he said, "in the fullness of time."

"Don't talk about work," asked Laz, "you'll put my blood pressure up." He laughed.

Dick nodded his head, "I'm sorry, by the way," he said. "I'm sorry I didn't make it to the funeral – I was in a fucking car accident would you believe!"

Laz stared at his friend blankly. "What funeral?" he asked.

Dick looked puzzled. "Why your's, of course..."

"Mine?" Laz shook his head slowly, thinking it must be his medication kicking in. "Mine? I'm not dead!"

"They didn't tell you?" Dick paled "Holy fuck, shit, Jesus Christ, stupid fuck..."

"Are you drunk?" asked Laz "what the fuck are you talking about? Funeral?"

"Fuck. They really didn't tell you..." Dick stammered. "Listen Laz, just forget I said anything. Yeah, I'm drunk... That's it! Stupid fucking drunk! Of course you're not dead, you're here aren't you?"

"Dick, don't mess with me. I'm on enough medication to kill an elephant. What the fuck are you talking about?"

"Oh Jeez... I'm sorry Laz, I thought you knew..." Dick reached for Laz's hand, not quite sure how to tell a friend that he has been seconds away from being barbecued alive. "They thought you were dead, Laz... you had a freaking funeral!"

"Are you crazy" said Laz, getting redder in the face.

"Laz, I thought you knew. The guy at the crematorium heard you moving around just before he pushed the button. They were about to fry you, or grill you, or whatever they do... Laz, you were one second away from eternity."

The numbers on the blood pressure monitor started to go down rapidly just as the digits on Laz's pulse monitor headed in the opposite direction. A loud insistent beeping started and red lights began to flash outside the door. Dick heard panicked footsteps running down the corridor towards them. "Crash team, 303, stat!" echoed throughout the center.

Dick stepped backwards into the bathroom.

"Oh my God!" he whispered to himself. "What have I done?" He heard a noise behind him and turned to see Stephen, seated on the toilet, pants down around his legs, controller in-hand and headphones on ears, his fingers madly dashing from one button to the other as he stole a Dodge Viper from some drug dealer in the 'hood, playing Grand Theft Auto.

In the end, the defibrillator paddles weren't needed, a few mils of adrenaline did the trick, and ten minutes later Laz was sitting up, just as he was before, except his face was a ghostly white.

"They thought I was dead" he muttered "they thought I was dead. They were going to burn me..."

Dick stood in the doorway of the bathroom wondering whether to say anything or just get the hell out of there before anyone could pin it on him. Behind him he heard a quiet voice. "My Mom is so going to kick your ass... "

"You OK, Laz? Dick ventured "you feeling alright now?"

"Dick, just get the fuck over here and tell me what happened," Laz commanded.

So Dick did, beginning with "Just be grateful you weren't embalmed Laz..."

"I wasn't even embalmed!" Laz cried. "That bitch wouldn't even have me fucking embalmed? Nice, really nice!"

THE FUNERAL REVISITED

"SO TELL ME about the funeral..."

Laz had been home for a week now and hadn't raised the issue with Mary or the kids. He figured he would bide his time, wait for the right moment and just starting evening dinner, with everyone in one place, gathered around the table somehow seemed to be it.

"Must have been pretty upsetting?" he speculated.

"Of course it was darling, we were distraught" Mary assured him "everyone was. It was such a shock... one minute you were there and the next minute... well, you were inside a body bag headed out the backdoor"

Laz dropped a carrot.

"Backdoor? They didn't take me out the front? I was lying the front hall wasn't I?"

"Well, I didn't want anyone to see. I didn't want to upset the neighbors, so I had them take the hearse around the back"

Laz sighed, "You'd think they'd take me out of the front door of my own house..."

Mary touched his arm. "But you weren't really dead Laz.

In a way, we've saved that moment for another time..."

"But you thought I was dead and took me out the fucking back!"

Mary looked sternly at him "Lazarus Finds, I will not have that language in front of the children!"

"Yeah, shut the fuck up" laughed Stephen.

"Stephen," equally stern look "do you want to lose your X-box?"

"Sorry!" Stephen responded contrite, in a none too convincing way.

"Sorry" added Laz, somewhat more sincerely. " Of course it doesn't matter which door they used. I was dead, I suppose"

"You were dear, you were" added Mary thinking of the twenty million dollars that she had already mentally spent before Lazarus was so cruelly snatched from eternity.

Lazarus pondered the whole scene in his imagination, the paramedics, the doctors, the undertaker. It made him feel rather important. He'd actually made CNN news, even though they had called him Les.

"You didn't have me embalmed?" he added aimlessly.

Mary coughed. "There seemed no point dear, and I hated the thought of your body having all that nasty, smelly formaldehyde being pumped through it..."

"I suppose" answered Lazarus "I suppose that didn't make a lot of sense."

"It didn't'" agreed Mary "it didn't!" relieved to have dodged that bullet.

Laz sighed. "What kind of casket did I have" he mused.

"A lovely white oak one darling" Mary nervously answered "simply beautiful... Gold handles..."

"Nice'" he said. "I like white oak"

"I knew you did dear," confirmed Mary. "That's why I choose it."

"Did you get a refund?"

"On what?"

"The coffin... You know, Craig's List 'one white oak coffin, slightly used, cheap to good home'" Laz jested and laughed for the first time in a long time.

"Wasn't really necessary" answered Mary noncommittally.

"What do you mean?" Laz asked, now puzzled.

"Mom rented it Dad" offered Stephen "you can get them by the hour..."

"You rented my coffin?"

"She could have got a steel one!" the boy added helpfully, 'or even gold!"

"Again darling, no point putting you in a $20,000 box and then burning it twenty minutes later..."

For once Laz couldn't disagree, he sighed, "I suppose"

"and we used that money to buy the horse" added Judith "so it didn't really cost us anything! Free horse!"

"You got the horse then?" he asked.

"Yes, he's lovely. Although he's not as good a jumper as they said he was..." advised Judith.

Lazarus could see another trade-in coming shortly. There was always a better, faster, higher-jumping horse on the horizon. He just wondered whether Judith ever improved her riding abilities herself? Whether it was like putting a learner driver into a Maserati or Ferrari and expecting them to win a Grand Prix. He wasn't going to spoil the evening by debating it. As soon as he did, Judith would be off to her room, slamming doors, crying on the phone to her boyfriend, stomping around above their heads. They would be treading on eggshells for days.

"And what about the service" asked Laz "was it nice?"

Mary and Judith glanced at each other, Stephen looked up "I have it on my iPhone if you want to watch it?"

THE RETURN

.

LAZ SAT WITH the iPhone in hand, staring sorrowfully at the display. "Stephen, can you show me how to replay this thing again please?" he asked.

"OK" said the boy "But hurry up! You must have watched it ten times already."

"It's not everyone one who get's to watch their own funeral," Mary interjected. "At least, unless they're watching from heaven, I suppose?" she added.

"Or in Judith's case, Hell!" suggested the boy.

"Stephen!" Laz admonished him, more from impatience than anything else, "just show me the video again…"

"I'm not sure they let you watch from Hell" Mary speculated. "They probably have rules against it.'

"And you stop it by pushing here," the boy demonstrated. "Not by pushing here. OK?"

Laz nodded, pressed his lips together and wondered why they made these things so damned difficult. He pushed the play button.

"Or maybe they make you wait until then before they tell you whether you're going to Heaven or not?" Mary suggested. "That would make sense."

"Probably…" muttered Laz, then asking "So where is Cousin Alfred" to no one in particular.

"He said he had a bad back" answered Mary. "He was worried he might be asked to be a pall bearer and thought it would look bad if he wasn't"

"Humph… " Laz grunted "How about Vinnie" referring to Mary's brother Vincent.

"He was booked on a cruise and couldn't get out of it…" she answered.

"He's a priest" cried Laz "what kind of a priest goes on a cruise?"

"He was going as a chaplain" she replied "He was really excited and didn't want to let the boys down…"

"Boys?" queried Laz.

"Boy Scouts" answered Mary "Outward Bound… Vinnie's had his name down forever?"

"Nobody from the Rotary Club?"

"I told them, but no one came" said Mary.

"Of course not!" replied Laz "First Monday of the Month! It's the monthly meeting and lunch!" He shook his head and sighed "Could you not even have scheduled it at two o'clock? They'd have been drunk by then… It would have been a great funeral!"

"Sorry!" said Mary indignantly "I'm supposed to schedule your funeral around your friends social schedule. Luckily, I'll know for next time!"

"And you say there was no one at all from work? No one?"

"I phoned them. They said Doug Dangle was going to come, but he had to leave at 11:30 for a lunch at the Union League. Dick and some HR people were supposed to be there, but never came. I wondered if some of those old ladies were maybe ex-employees of yours, but remembered they weren't really your type," Mary added with a sneer.

"Thirteen people" Laz shook his head slowly from side to side "only thirteen people..."

"Well nine really" answered Stephen "If you don't count the old ladies who didn't know you, and the black girl who was at the wrong funeral, and add in yourself..."

"Not even Dick and Aubrey..." Laz added wistfully.

"Told them too, at the club" answered Mary "no one came. You think they would after all the money you've poured down your throat there. You think they'd buy you a gold coffin with hot and cold single malt!"

Laz shook his head from side to side, handed the iPhone back to his son and then staggered to his feet.

"I'm going out" said Lazarus.

"You can't drive" said Mary "and I'm too busy to take you. My show's on in a minute!"

"I'll get a cab, don't worry," said Laz. "I'll be fine."

"Where are you going" she asked adding "dear" as an after thought.

"To the club" said Laz "I want to find out why the Hell they didn't come to my funeral!"

"Is that wise" asked Mary "Shall I call them?"

"Don't you dare" Laz told her "I want to surprise them!"

Laz arrived at the club a little after six in the evening. Just about the time he would have done normally, back before the events on that night. It looked warm and welcoming. He could imagine settling down in a deep leather chair and relaxing with a bourbon on the rocks, soaking in the glow of the huge fire, letting the alcohol start to calm him down and take him away from this nightmare. He should have come before. Laz almost leapt up the stairs, well as much as a man recovering from several broken limbs could do, but he did in his mind.

Sloanes, or Soames, the doorman opened the grand portal and Laz embraced the sanctuary as he walked through it. It was all there, just as he remembered. The sweeping staircase, the rich mahogany panelling, the smell of wood smoke and money, the sense of refuge and escape. He could see Aubrey at the far end of the bar and started to walk towards him.

"Excuse me Sir" came a voice from behind him, "excuse me. Can I help you?" It was Parker the club secretary. Laz stared at him blankly. "Can I help you?" he asked again.

"It's me Parker, " exclaimed Laz. " Me. Lazarus Finds..."

"I'm well aware who you are Mr Finds," answered Parker. "I'm merely asking how I can be of service?"

"Oh, sorry" answered Laz. "Thank you. I was just going through to the Member's Bar."

"I'm afraid you cannot do that Mr Finds." Parker stared at the confused and now very tired man in front of him. "For you are no longer a member."

"I'm what?" exclaimed Laz. "Of course I am. I'm paid up through June!"

"You are no any longer, Sir," the secretary sighed. "For when your wife called to advise us of your, so-called, demise. She cancelled said membership and demanded a refunding of any dues not yet expired."

"She what?" cried Laz.

"Which is not something we normally do. Normally the member's widow kindly donates the remaining dues to the club or one of its charities. But she insisted on a full refund," he continued then smiling. "And since it was you

Mr Finds, we made an exception."

"But, but..." stammered Laz, "I'll write you a check now –
and pay you back. I'll take out a new full year. Two
years…"

Parker drew himself up to his full height, a good six inches
taller than the now former member hunched over before
him.

"Unfortunately that would have to go before the
membership committee Mr Finds, as you are no longer a
member, and we now have a long waiting list and we are,
how can I put this delicately?" he thought for a moment
and then, as if inspired, added "Ah yes, we are much more
selective that we once were."

"Preposterous!' cried Laz. "I've been a member for nineteen
years! This is ridiculous. Let me see Aubrey, he'll sort this
out."

"Mr Aubrey has told me to tell you Mr. Finds, were you to
call, that he is indisposed..."

"But he's at the bar!" pointed Laz. "I can see him..."

Parker sighed. "He is at the bar Sir. At the bar, and
indisposed."

Lazarus started to make for the Brandywine Room
hurriedly, at least as best he could considering the crutches,
but a large hand caught him on the shoulder causing him to
scream in pain and nearly fall over as he was swiveled

around   like a top by the uniformed man.

"I'll just have you shown out now, Sir!" barked Parker. "
And please do not make to repeat this scene again. The
club has gotten over your departure and so now Sir, must
you."

As he was hustled toward the, now most unwelcoming
doors, Lazarus noticed a new entry on the plaque denoting
"Deceased Members Not Forgotten." Scripted in gold leaf,
the most recent entry read 'Les Finds'.

The door was opened and the doorman pitched him out
quite unceremoniously but with a growl. "Goodnight Sir.
And my name is Soames, you miserable little turd."

THE CHURCH

LAZARUS WAS BACK at St Peter's. He hadn't felt this depressed since he was lying here dead.

It's bad enough, he thought to himself, when you are having a party and the time comes, the one as posted on the invite, and no one is there. But you know that eventually, sooner or later even, people will come. Some just didn't want to be the first to arrive, others like to come later and make an entrance. However, funerals are different. Like football matches they kick off at a prescribed time. They're expected to last an hour or so, unless they go into extra time with an over long eulogy. But for the most part they are pretty predictable. So why did so few people come, he wanted to know?

Many times Laz had laid awake actually imagining his own funeral. His first thought and concern was that the church would not be big enough to hold the vast crowd that would want to come. His second concern was that Mary would already have died before him and she not get to see this grand turnout nor would she be there to weep helplessly beside the coffin or possibly, when his imagination really ran away with him, throw herself prostrate upon it, fall in front of it, try and open it – all the time wailing hysterically.

But now he had seen the video. He had the eyewitness account. There was almost nobody. Worst still, his daughter was on the phone most of the time, his wife looked like she was waiting for a bus checking her watch every thirty seconds, his son, if he wasn't filming the proceedings, was probably playing video games throughout. The only person who seemed genuinely upset was Mr Patel from the Firestone dealership, which reminded Laz that he must check and see whether the Audi or the Mercedes were due their annual inspections soon. The church was, for all intents and purposes, empty.

From his work, Yours Mutual, there was no one. No senior management, none of his direct reports, none of those pretty PAs he was always so complementary to, not the mailroom staff to whom he gave a big box of biscuits to every Christmas (if only to ensure he got his packages on time the rest of the year), none of them.

Mary assured him that she had let the company know immediately and they had even sent a motorcycle courier around to collect his office keys. But none of them seemed to care enough to show up. To pay their respects. To pay homage. Could it be that they just didn't care? Had they gotten the time wrong? Did Mary give them the wrong time, just to get back at him?

He had been sitting there about twenty minutes when the young priest tentatively approached him.

"Can I help you? I'm Father Sam Pratt..."

"No, no! Don't worry about me. I was just sitting here thinking," Laz assured him.

There was a bit of a silence and then the priest edged in and sat next to him. "For sure," he said, "thinking is good. And this is a great place for thinking. No one to bother you. No distractions. No TV. I do a lot of thinking here myself."

Laz wanted to say, "Well piss off and leave me to think then." Though he thought it would be wrong to swear in the church. Plus it was the priest's church after all Instead he just said, "Yes it is"

They sat there, the two of them, together. Looking up at the altar. Looking down at their feet resting on the kneeling bench. It went on for a long time.

"About what?"

"Sorry?" said Laz. "What about what?"

"You're thinking," said the priest. " About what?"

Lazarus had come here for solitude, not the third degree, but he recognized it was in the priest's nature and he couldn't help it. He remembered a story from his youth, he thought it was Confucius who perhaps had first told it, about a scorpion who had asked a frog to carry him across the river and so help him get to the other side. Or maybe he'd heard it on Kung Fu?

"But you'll sting me" said the frog.

"Why would I do that?" answered the scorpion. "If I sting you, then you will die and drown and so will I. We would then both drown and die."

*So they made a pact, and the frog agreed to carry the
scorpion across the swollen river. Halfway across the river
the scorpion stung the frog.*

*"Why did you do that?" cried the frog. "Now we will both
die".*

*"I don't know?" said the scorpion. "I suppose it's just in
my nature," And then they both drowned.*

"So what is it that troubles you, my son?"

Lazarus sighed. A deep sigh. He hadn't planned on
unburdening himself, but why did he come here? He didn't
believe in God. Mary and he attended church rarely,
Christmas, christenings, weddings and, now, funerals. The
most recent being his own.

"Father, do you remember doing a funeral here – about six
weeks ago?"

"I do a lot of funerals, my son," answered the priest.

"You'd remember this one," said Laz, looking up into the
eyes of the priest. "I was the dead guy!"

The priest looked puzzled for just a second and then
recoiled. "You were the man who was still alive!" he
exclaimed. "Jesus, Mary and St. Joseph! You're Mr. Finds!
It was a miracle. I was just telling my mother about it the
other day. One minute you're dead, next minute you're
banging on the box. A miracle!"

"Or a misdiagnosis?" volunteered Laz.

"But it was quite remarkable," insisted Father Sam, "you were snatched away from death by the fingertips! You were even on CNN!"

"I was indeed," said Lazarus. "Indeed. You'd think I was very lucky."

There was a very long pause. Laz slowly looked around him. Here at eight o'clock at night the church probably had more people in it that were at his farewell. He shook his head. He choked and tears started to course down his cheeks.

"What is wrong, Mr. Finds?" asked the priest. "What could cause you to feel so sad?"

Laz shook his head.

"You cheated death! You should feel glorious, invincible," offered Father Sam.

"I wish I hadn't woken up!" muttered Laz. "I wish I'd been burned up that day. At least I would have gone to the hereafter without knowing what I know now."

THE PRIEST

FIFTEEN MINUTES LATER Lazarus was in the priest's office being offered a large whiskey. "I find it helps." said Sam.

Laz looked the glass, smelled it, imagined the Glens of Scotland from whence the whiskies blended within had been at least twenty years in the making. "You know?" he said. "I haven't had a drink in months now. Not since they first took me to the hospital, since I fell down the stairs. I feel that if I took a sip now, I feel I would be condemning myself once and for all."

"Then you shouldn't!" said the priest. "If that's how you feel. For an addiction to the bottle is a terrible thing. I've seen it tear families apart," he explained. "Lose men their jobs, their pride, their whole reason for living. Sure it can be the road to unmitigated disaster." The priest lifted the glass away from Laz and poured the contents into his own. "And this is Johnnie Walker Blue Label and it would be wasted on a man who wouldn't appreciate it," he concluded.

Laz looked down at his once bulging waist, now slimmed from not drinking alcohol and from eating better food and doing so at the right time of day, not stuffing himself with cheesesteaks from Pat's or Geno's as an afterthought at the end of a long drinking session. "I feel," said Laz. "I feel like that has been part of my problem all along."

The priest nodded, slowly sipping the Johnnie Blue and smiling. "Go on" he said at last.

"I feel like, for me, the drink was an escape. A painkiller, if you like. Something to make me forget what was going on around me." Father Sam nodded, enjoying the burn of the Scotch.

"And the drugs, of course?" suggested Father Sam trying to be helpful.

"Oh I would never do drugs!" said Laz "too complicated. Too seedy, illegal and too difficult to get a fix when you need it. There one thing about the booze, at least there's always a bar open some place."

"I see," agreed the priest, but he didn't. The parishioners in his previous church never seemed to have that problem. They seemed to be stoned all the time.

"No, the booze was my downfall," Laz continued. "I'd have a bottle of something in the office, just to keep me going until I got to the club, and then the club 'til bedtime. Maybe a swift one when I got home. A nightcap you know?"

"And what about your family?" asked Sam.

"Oh, it seemed we drifted apart years ago." answered Laz. "Yes, we still lived together, live together even now of course, and that. It's not like I was running around having affairs and such. I just kind of stopped being there."

"Physically?" suggested the priest. Laz nodded.

"Physically? Yes," he said. "But emotionally too." Laz thought for a moment as the priest sipped again. "But not just with them," he confessed, "with everyone, with everything."

"Well, you have a chance to change that now," said Father Sam. "You've realized what you've got, what you've done and where you've been and you are coming out of the other side," he said with hope.

"It's too late Father, too late," protested Laz. "Didn't you see how no one came out to my funeral? There was hardly any one there."

"Well, you were hardly in pole position to count them now, were you?" said the priest.

"I have a video," said Laz gloomily, thrusting Stephen's iPhone into the priest's hands. "I have the whole thing on tape, or file, or whatever. Look at this..." He pressed play. "My wife, my sister, my two kids and then..." his throat caught, "and then, strangers."

"Will you look at that?" said the priest. "That's incredible. Who could believe it? It's a movie camera in a phone! Isn't that just amazing?"

"It's an iPhone, Father," said Laz testily. "Have you not seen one before?"

"Well, of course I've seen them," the priest rebuked him. "I've seen them. I've seen the people in the congregation tapping them and talking into them. But movies! Will you get a load of that?"

"If you'd just watch the video, Father." Laz pleaded with him. "You'll see what I mean. The church is empty!"

"Well, I know the church was empty, my son," said Father Pratt. "Your funeral, well your service, set me behind all day long. You see, your wife had me delay it twenty minutes. She too was convinced we were going to be needing the overflow room and the loudspeakers outside and all of the gear for the big mass. It was all laid out. Just like when Mrs Murphy died."

Laz had a mental vision of hundreds of people unable to get in to the funeral service, but it wasn't his mass. "Who was Mrs Murphy?" he ventured.

"Ah sure, you couldn't go competing with Eileen Murphy now," consoled the priest. "Sure, she was the crossing guard at the school here for forty years. Jeepers, we must've had nearly a thousand people here."

"A thousand?" repeated Laz. "For a crossing guard?"

"More, I'd wager, if I was a betting man," mused Father Platt. "They had to close Lancaster Avenue for three hours."

"Now that's my what I was expecting!" cried Laz. "I wanted her funeral!"

"I see," said the priest. "So that's what this is all about is it? I suppose you'd imagined a bigger turnout had you? Well, that's often the case. We can't all be Mrs Murphy's you know. Mind you, it's not like most of us can come back and complain about it," he concluded.

"Father?" said Laz trying to put it in simple terms for the cleric. "I'd worked twenty odd years for a company with one thousand plus employees! Four hundred and thirty two of them worked for me. Not one of them came."

The priest slowly shook his head.

"I spent every night at a club with seven hundred odd members. None of them came either. "

"Is that the Union League" asked the priest.

"No, it's the other one" replied Laz, shaking his head.

"Pity," said the priest. "I'm trying to get in there."

"Father Sam, my own mother didn't even show up! I could've had…" Laz quickly did the math, "nearly eighteen hundred people!"

The priest played the video again, if only to buy himself some time. He seemed to have no trouble figuring it out now, thought Laz, and he'd never seen one five minutes ago. True, the congregation was pitifully small, Father Sam thought, but he had held funerals when no one showed up. Sometimes there just was no one left to remember you, no one to grieve for you or for themselves. Old people who just laid in their beds hoping to die, praying to die. He saw them everyday on his visits to the retirement and nursing homes. He'd often thought, as a priest, he was at least guaranteed a reasonable turnout at his send off whenever his Maker called him. But he sure as heck wouldn't be around to complain if he didn't. At least, he hoped he wouldn't.

Laz looked over the top of the iPhone. "Who are these people?" he gestured with his finger. "I don't even know these people."

"Well," ventured Father Pratt. "That is Mrs Harcher. She's eighty-seven, she does the flowers. A lovely lady. she used to do the accounts before her eyes went."

He paused the screen and pointed to another elderly figure. "And this is Miss Bowles, she loves a good funeral and a nice cry. This is Mr Thompson, judging by the shopping bags he was on his was back from the supermarket and popped in to get warm. He's not that religious, treats the church as more of a social club." He looked over the phone at Laz. "We have Bingo, Tuesdays and Fridays," he said brightly, "You should come!"

The other man shook his head. "Don't you see, Father?" pleaded Laz. "Nobody cares, nobody came. Not even my best friend."

"What about this girl?" asked the priest. "The black one? Is she from your work?"

"Never seen her before," said Laz. He looked closer. "Is she crying? She at least seems upset."

"We all have our problems," said Sam. "Look at how she runs out of there. A troubled soul, if I ever saw one. I hope she wasn't stealing something," added the priest.

Sam finished the Scotch and walked around the desk. He patted Laz on the shoulder, a reassuring pat. "Go and talk to your family. Talk to your friends. Ask them 'Why?' Maybe this experience will take you on a new road? Maybe at your next funeral..." he chuckled. Laz looked up at the priest, expecting wisdom.
"Well, who knows?" Father Pratt concluded, thinking, but not saying, that if Mrs Harcher, Miss Bowles and Mr Thompson had passed on by then, well, there could be even less souls in that congregation.

THE REALIZATION

LAZARUS TRIED TO talk to Mary that night.

He had limped home exhausted. For some ridiculous
reason he thought that a walk back from the church to the
house might help clear his head, but he had under estimated
the stress he was placing on his still healing limbs.
Halfway home his legs started to ache with every step, and
to make matters worse, trying to use the crutches just made
his injured arm burn like it was being seared with a hot
poker. Even though it was a cold March night, perspiration
soon soaked through his shirt and then his jacket and into
his raincoat. His underarms started to chaff unbearably.

Laz reached a point where he could go no more and
searched for the iPhone, only to find that the incessant
playing and replaying of the funeral video by the priest had
exhausted the battery and it was now totally dead.
Waynesborough Road was lonely and dark and Laz tried to
flag down a few of the cars that passed him with his good
crutch arm, but they either didn't see him or decided he was
a nut. Something he would probably agree with, had he
been in their warm and cozy sedans and SUVs. He plodded
on as best he could, rueing his decision not to call a cab
from Father Sam's office, when from behind he heard a low
crunch of gravel and the slowing of a vehicle. "A ride!" he
thought.

From a loudspeaker boomed a voice. "Drop the crutches

and raise your hands…"

Laz considered the ridiculousness of the instructions and started to turn towards the bright light now being shone upon him from behind.

"Don't move!" said the voice. "Just drop the crutches and raise your hands," it repeated.

Laz was certain that there were many municipalities in the United States where the IQ of the average police officer was well above that of the local citizenry. Lower Wayne was not one of those municipalities, whether by sheer bad luck or design, the local township seemed to go for good customer service, like rescuing dogs and cats and bringing home drunk teenagers, rather than well-honed policing skills.

"If I drop the crutches," Laz shouted back. "I'll fall over!"

Laz could hear a couple of officers discussing the predicament between themselves, but they still seemed unconvinced he was not about to make a run for it.

"Could you sit on the ground with your hands up?" a new voice shouted.

Laz looked down at the road, made wet from the run off from the melting snow and the earlier downpour. "Not without hurting myself and getting very wet,'" he shouted back to them.

Another discussion took place between the officer before a

compromise was finally reached.

"How about," shouted the first, "you kind of lean on the crutches but stick your hands up in the air from your elbows?"

Laz thought about it. "Like this?" he shouted back trying the suggested pose, albeit a bit wobbly, that the first officer came up with.

"Yeah, yeah!" came the reply enthusiastically. "That's good! Now hold that…"

Presently, a Lower Wayne police sergeant appeared in front of him shining a flashlight in his face. Laz couldn't see much of him, except that he was peering at him.

"Say, is that you Mr Finds?" said the officer.

"It's me" responded Laz, hoping he should be relieved by the recognition.

"Why didn't you say?" said the policeman. "It's me. Officer Frye. Let's get you into the car. We've had a lot of calls about you!"

"From Mary?" asked Laz hopefully, as the two policemen took the crutches from him and carefully aided him back to the cruiser.

"No, just from people driving along," replied the policeman. "Saying there's some lunatic walking around in Lower Wayne. You don't often see that you know, people walking, especially on crutches…"

"Yeah, well," responded Laz. "There's a first time for everything."

When they got him home, Mary had had a couple of glasses of Chardonnay already and was getting ready to watch American Idol.

Officer Frye explained what had happened and Mary just looked at Laz like an annoying toddler who had wandered off in the supermarket during a shopping trip. She sent him into the front room. "Before you go Officer," she asked quietly. "I need some advice."

The policeman looked around, aware that the lady had something of a sensitive nature to share with him.

"Yes, Ma'am" he whispered. "Anything."

Mary looked down at the floor. "You haven't got any tips, have you?"

"Tips, Ma'am?" he answered, slightly confused.

"Tips, ideas, advice…" Mary prompted. "You must surely come across them in going about your day-to-day business."

Officer Frye was perplexed. "I would just keep a close eye on him, I guess Ma'am," he suggested, as best he felt able. "Mr Finds has been through an awful lot these past few…" The policeman didn't get to finish, before Mary suddenly cut him off.

"Not Laz, you numbskull"! she cried. "I mean that!" She pointed to the faded, but still obvious white, outline of a distorted body on the black slate floor of the foyer. "How do I get that out?"

Officer Frye went beet-red and looked fit to explode, but she didn't give him a chance. "I mean, you're the one who's put it there. You must have an idea how to get rid of it?" Mary looked at him sternly. "I'd hate to think this little matter was going to come between us and the Hunt's support of the Officer's charities this year. So I suggest you get your CSI people working on it, pronto!"

The policeman tried to protest, but she already had him halfway through the door. "Have your CSI people call me," she shouted after him as she closed it and headed back to the television.

Mary was devoted to American Idol. It was a show she made sure she never missed. She had seen every series right from the very first one, though she now felt Kelly Clarkson wouldn't stand a chance these days. Today, her friends all watched it too, but she knew she had been the first to discover it and she felt a special ownership for that. She also had to watch it 'live,' never on the DVR, lest one of her friends should call with a comment or, worst still, the result.

She was pulling for Darren this year. He was cuter than all the others and had a great body. He might be gay, she wasn't quite sure. She had been so disappointed by Adam

Lambert, a few years ago, so she tried not to think about it. Plus Darren had quite a good voice, even if they hadn't packaged him properly yet. She had the phone at hand for the vote when it came, and turned away any calls that arrived during the show in case they interfered with her ability to start calling in. She managed to get twenty minutes into this episode before Laz decided to open up about his evening.

"Mary" ventured Laz, "I've been thinking..."

"Ummm?" came the response. "Not now Darling. Simon's going to tear this one apart..."

"I've been thinking about my life, our world, the family. Everything," he continued regardless.

"Ummm, that's good," she answered, half holding up her hand and keeping her attention strictly focused on Felicia.

"It's just," he ventured, "I think I've let you all down a bit..."

Mary nodded. "That's nice dear," she agreed. "Look at Felicia, she looks terrified..."

"Mary, I'm trying to talk to you. This is important!"

"No Laz! This is the semi-final. This is important!" she answered threatening to throw the remote control at him.

Laz didn't want to push the issue too much, but he knew The Amazing Race was on next and that wouldn't make things any easier.

"I think I could have been a much better husband," he continued on blindly.

Mary pushed the pause button, she could catch up in the commercials she thought.

"Stop the presses everyone!" she cried. "My husband has been hit by lightening. What the hell are you talking about?"

"I think, I could have been better to you, to Stephen and, well, even to Judith."

"Well, duh!" suggested Mary. "I think that's been pretty obvious to everyone for what, the last twenty years or so? What brought this on?"

"I went to see Father Pratt," Lazarus confessed.

"Oh that idiot?" cried Mary. "No wonder you're messed up."

"What do you mean by that?" he questioned, puzzled.

Mary wasn't really in a position to elaborate on her much considered opinion that if the blessed priest had given a shorter sermon, instead of prattling on about someone he had never met before, the crematorium deed might well have been concluded many minutes earlier. Laz would be gone. She would have had her insurance money and could have started her new life by now. As it turned out, thanks to the priest, she couldn't even watch her favorite TV show without him reminding her what might have been.

"Nothing," sighed Mary. "I just don't like these new priests."

Laz swallowed. "He, Father Pratt, um, Father Sam, thinks I should start again. Try to put things right. Right with you, right with the kids, with work and stuff."

Mary looked him squarely in the eyes whilst mentally calculating how long the program had been paused and whether she could catch up to real time before one of her friends called to gush or complain about Simon's final verdict. Because it really was all about Simon. She could hear a clock ticking down the available seconds in her head.

"Laz,'" she said as patiently as she could. "We're a long way down the road from this. Things haven't been good for a long time. Whatever relationship we once had, has come down to just living in the same house." She thought a small smile might help him realize it was for the best and time to get back to Idol.

Lazarus started to cry a little.

"Oh God!" she exclaimed. "Don't do that. At least you were always a man, don't turn into blubberer."

He swallowed hard. "I just think we should try and salvage this. For us, for the kids."

Mary figured she now only had twenty seven seconds, so she gave it to him straight. "Lazarus, you make a good living, you look after us. The kids are nearly grown. When they go, we'll discuss this again, but our relationship is not going to change because you fell down the stairs while drunk. It may have fucked up your life, but it surely isn't going to fuck up mine. Now, if you don't mind..." and she pushed 'play' on the remote.

"By the way," she added as by way of an afterthought. "Clarence called you from your HR people. They want you to go in tomorrow."

THE RETURN

LAZ WASN'T USED to sitting in the reception area of the Yours Mutual Human Resources department. Normally, he would have just walked through the entrance, swiped his card at the electronic wall pad, pushed the door and headed straight for Clarence Causley's office to demand a new assistant; that a salesman be sacked; that he be allowed some extra perk on his expenses.

This morning, however, Laz had tried to use his ID card on the door and it hadn't worked. All that happened was the pad emitted a very negative and uninviting sounding buzz that indicated there was a problem with him gaining entry through that door and the flashing display above the pad advised him, and anyone else in sight, 'Access Is Denied'. Laz imagined they must have re-issued the cards in his absence, but he would soon have them put that right. He had been on sick leave for over three months now, so it wasn't surprising and now, he tried to to convince himself, he was looking forward to getting back into 'the fray'.

"Can I help you?" a receptionist, who looked about sixteen, asked him from a desk that he had never noticed before.

Laz regarded her with distain. "I have an appointment with Clarence" he told her shortly.

She looked at a list of appointments and then back at Lazarus. "Name?" she asked him.

"Lazarus Finds," he responded as politely as he could and sighed. He didn't remember her, but then he hadn't noticed the desk before either, he thought. The girl ticked him off an unseen list and then handed him a clipboard.

"Fill in the application on the front, don't forget the back," she said. Then looking him up and down whispered, "Make sure you do the 'Disabilities' section on page four." She looked around and added conspiratorially, "You'll have a much better chance!"

It took Laz a couple of seconds to understand what the girl was saying to him before he exploded. "I'm not here for a goddamn fucking job," he clarified rather loudly. "I'm the Senior Vice Fucking President of Sales! Now tell Clarence to get out the hell out here!"

The girl shrank before his eyes and he felt a mild glow of satisfaction that he still could muster such energy, that he still had the power to make the minions quiver. But then, as he continued to stare at her, he thought she looked like she might cry, and then she did start to wipe her eyes as she gamely she picked up the phone, pushed a few buttons and spoke some words into the mouthpiece. She turned back towards her visitor. "He's coming," she told him very quietly, her face bright red and the rest of her body shaking and on the verge of breaking down.

Laz wanted to apologize but wasn't sure what words to use and before he could figure it out Clarence strove urgently through the double glass doors. "Laz, come on in…" he almost yelled. "Where have you been? I've missed you,

you Son-of-a-gun!" He ushered Laz through the doors while giving the receptionist an apologetic wave with his free hand.

"Sorry about that…" said Laz indicating the girl.

"Don't worry," said Clarence. "She's new. Probably had'nt heard of you."

"I tried my card..." Laz tried to explain.

"Should work, should've worked. No problem, we'll have that taken care of. Come right this way." Clarence guided him towards his corner office.

Las was relieved and followed Clarence to the office. It was the same one he used to storm into whenever he was upset about, well, anything really. Clarence had always been a bit of a sounding board and it helped Laz to go in there, tell Clarence the latest reason why he was quitting, scream and shout about Doug Dangle, the CEO, know that eventually Clarence would calm him down and tell him how vital he, 'Lazarus Finds,' was to the everyday success and long-term plans of Yours Mutual and Laz always knew he would leave there feeling well-vented and a whole lot better about his future. It was like getting a massage, but significantly cheaper, he always thought.

"So Laz?" smiled Clarence. "How are you?"

Lazarus eyed the pile of paper that Clarence placed in front of himself.

"I am fine," he answered slowly, moving the crutch that he had first leaned against Clarence's desk down onto the floor in front of him and out of the HR director's line of sight. "Can't say I've never been better, but I'm getting better. Much better!"

"Excellent, excellent," Clarence said in a soothing tone. "So pleased to hear it. It must have been a quite shock?"

"Oh my word," said Lazarus, "such a shock! Can you imagine waking up in a coffin? In front of a crematorium oven..!" Laz couldn't actually remember any of that, but he felt he should weave it into every recollection of the events and every time he had done so it had become a more significant detail in the story.

"Oh that" said Clarence. "Yes, shocking! Absolutely shocking! I'm surprised you didn't drop dead of a heart attack when you found out!" the HR guy laughed.

Laz didn't laugh however, instead he looked at the pile of papers in front of Clarence that he was finding equally as shocking.

"So Clarence, when can I come back to work?" Lazarus asked. "I'm ready..." Even though he knew that he probably wasn't.

The head of human resources shuffled the papers, putting some to the back, others to the front, then reversing that and putting some new ones in the middle.

"Ah" he said, and then thought for a moment. "There

could be a tiny bit of a problem there, buddy!"

"How so?" asked Laz.

"Well, first of all…" Clarence continued "Had you, um, noticed you hadn't been receiving your regular paychecks since the, um, accident?"

Laz thought for a few moments. Doing the accounts had never ever been at the forefront of his mind even when he was working, and the basics; the mortgage, the credit cards, the school fees were all paid directly from the bank and tended to take care of themselves. "Um, no." he answered Clarence. "Why?"

"Well, let's go back..." Clarence suggested with some degree of hesitation. "When we first received word of your, um, your death, Doug felt that we needed to act quickly and decisively, needed to ensure there was a firm hand on the tiller and all that. Didn't want the sales force to get too jittery or start defecting to the Pru or Allstate or whatever."

Laz nodded slowly.

"Doug, no, we," Clarence corrected himself. "We all knew how you had built that team up over the last twenty years and we wanted to make sure that we kept it in tact, and kept our brightest stars away from the competition."

Laz groaned, they've only gone and given them all huge raises he thought to himself, and as for bright stars most of them were blithering idiots. Truth be told, the majority of them were just servicing accounts that Laz himself had brought in, set up and nurtured over the years.

"So what have you done?" asked Laz nervously. "Did you give them all a shit load of money?"

Clarence shifted nervously in his seat. "No, um, as for the sales force we did nothing. Doug was more concerned with showing them there would be continuity from day one on the management side," the HR guy explained.

"So that means what, precisely?" Laz asked, confused now.

"Well, Laz, I'm glad you asked me that" replied Clarence, clearly not glad at all. "You see... Doug suggested we acted immediately, so..." Clarence wiped his brow before continuing, "so, we replaced you."

"Replaced me!" Laz almost shouted, "replaced me with who, with what?"

Clarence swallowed again. "With someone Doug has been very impressed with of late, we, um, he replaced you with Leanne... Your deputy"

Lazarus sat up very straight, or as straight as he could manage, and tried to speak in the clearest most commanding voice he could, well, command. "Well, tell him to, un-replace me."

Clarence frowned a sad face, and waited a moment or two, as if he were a father about to tell his child that their hamster had just died. "I do so feel bad about this," he said, "and Doug anticipated you may say that, but that's just not possible. You see, we've given Leanne the job and she's moved a whole new team in." Then, as if it might help, Clarence added. "We gave her a huge raise!" It didn't.

"But what about my job!" demanded Laz. "I still have a job here, right?"

Clarence smiled, a sweet smile, but an HR smile. "Technically" and then he paused as if to mull it over. "Technically, um, you don't."

"But I'm not dead, Clarence." Laz protested, "You made a mistake."

"Again, technically," Clarence advised the now slumping Laz, "we didn't make a mistake. You made a mistake, or rather your doctors did, and we acted on their diagnosis. More than that – we acted on a death certificate that said you were, well, dead." He paused again, "in black and white..."

Laz tried to absorb what was happening, trying to figure out how he could turn any of this to his advantage, without losing his temper.

"So you're telling me that I no longer have a job here?"

"Once we got the death certificate, which Mary very kindly hand delivered by the way, we terminated your contract, paid three months salary into your bank account as a goodwill gesture, and, well, moved on..." smiled Clarence.

"But you'll be giving me a proper settlement, surely?" Laz demanded. "After nearly twenty-five years service?"

"If we had let you go, we certainly would have. Though don't quote me on that!" the HR director laughed. "Doug would cut off my balls for saying something like that, but since we were given a death certificate saying you were dead, well there was no need you see..."

Laz sat back, as he had done so may times before in this office when he felt things weren't quite going his way, and laughed. "Clarence, this is silly! I'm not dead, I'm here. Ready to pick up the reins where I left off. You won't even know I was gone." He smiled hopefully at the HR executive.

Clarence smiled back, that practiced human resource smile that says 'I'm on your side, but my hands are tied'. "The thing is Laz, about the reins… Doug kind of feels you dropped them quite a long time ago. In fact, now that Leanne picked them up, so to speak, sales look to be up eight percent this quarter already."

"Clarence, please!" Laz begged.

"And people have stopped quitting," Clarence continued, "and others, good salesmen who had left, have started to ask if they could come back." He shrugged, "all because of Leanne."

Laz had had enough of this. "OK, let me see Doug!"

Clarence shook his head, "Doug said he doesn't want to see

you."

Laz did menacing. "I said, let me see Doug!"

"And he said if you were to ask a second time I was to call Security," Clarence informed him.

Laz had long had a habit of saying the wrong thing at the wrong time and something inside him told him that this was one of those moments in one's life that to do so could have lasting repercussions. He chose his words very carefully.

"Clarence, I've had a long history with this company," he said. "I've devoted my entire career to it. And I had a terrible accident, one that nearly killed me, twice actually. So I suggest to you, that I am an employee coming back to his job after that fact and entitled to recommence his position being now fit and able (not that Laz actually felt either of those), or, if I am 'dead' as you so consider me to be, then I must be a "dead" person and so entitled to his life insurance."

"But..." said Clarence before he was cut off.

"But me no but's, Mr Causley" said Lazarus, "it's either one thing or the other and" he said leaning much closer to the HR director "if it takes an entire firm of lawyers to convince you and Doug Dangle and Dick Posman and all the rest of those SOBs of that, then that is the route I shall take and gladly foot you with the bill when I have convinced the courts of the Commonwealth of Pennsylvania of such."

Clarence gasped a little, as a goldfish would do when suddenly evacuated from a fishbowl, waiting for its owner to swoop it back into its tank again.

"I'll be in touch" said Laz "hopefully we won't have to go that far..." and he walked as stridently as he could out of the room. It was only when he was through the electronically guarded doorway he realized his crutch was still under the desk in Clarence's office. He looked at the girl on the reception. She sniffed at him and looked away.

It was going to be a long and painful journey home.

THE ACCOUNTING

"FIRED!" SAID MARY. "Fired? How the hell can you be fired? You haven't been at work for the last three months!"

"Well, not fired exactly." Laz tried to explain, not quite understanding it himself, "replaced, I suppose. After dying in service," he added, trying to be helpful.

"But you're not dead, you idiot!" Mary clarified for him. "Though sometimes you do act as though you are."

Laz was a little annoyed that he was taking all the heat for this when, to his recollection, Mary had precipitated this whole thing. "Well, perhaps if you hadn't run right over there waving my death certificate in their faces screaming, 'Lazarus is dead, Lazarus is dead! Show me the money…' this might never have happened!" he exclaimed.

Mary fixed him with a steely look. It was the dangerous loo. The look he had seen many times before and he knew to avoid engaging it. Laz made a mental note of where he'd positioned the replacement crutches in case he had to attempt a quick getaway, to the bathroom or some other place with a solid lock.

"Are you seriously suggesting I did that for the money, Lazarus?" Mary asked.

He shook his head, but kept silent.

"Did it not occur to you that, even in my grief, my first thought was for our children? That I should ensure that their father's employer should know he had passed away…"

Laz shook his head, hoping that was the response Mary desired.

"That your children should see you accorded the maximum respect due to you, for your lengthy service by that company…"

Laz nodded.

His wife hadn't finished. "That your company should be allowed to reach out, permitted to share in our grief, in our suffering" Mary demanded.

"I suppose," Laz agreed. "Except," he dared to say "Clarence said he had had to get a copy of the death certificate from Claims. That you didn't deliver one to him direct, he said"

"Isn't it the same" Mary asked innocently?

"Claims is off Walnut, down a small alley," Laz advised her cautiously. "We make it rather hard to find, on purpose. Head Office is on Market Street. Apparently, Clarence said he didn't know I'd "died" until a fraud check came through on the Wednesday morning, informing him that a current employee was trying to claim on his life policy."

"See!" cried Mary "triumphantly. I knew the system would get the information to the right people eventually!"

"And that's when he got the word out to the rest of the team," continued Laz, "that I had died on the Monday."

A silence fell between them for many moments as Laz hoped for some explanation from Mary, but always knew none would be coming.

"They still didn't come though Laz, did they!" Mary eventually added spitefully. "They still didn't come to your funeral. Not one of them! What did he say about that?"

"He said, 'I was through', Mary" Laz confirmed, "'finished'. No more office, no more parking spot, no more lovely salary, bonus or those sales conventions in the Caribbean that you hated so much!"

Mary glared at him. "Then how the hell are we going to live if you don't have a job?" she demanded fumbling with her iPhone.

Laz shrugged. "We'll have to find a way. This can't be the end with Yours Mutual. I'm sure they'll see sense one way or the other..."

Mary focused on the phone before eventually demanding. "Have you checked how much is in the bank account?"

Laz shrugged again and then maneuvered his crutch a little closer.

"Well I just did, dimwit!" said Mary. "Practically nothing…"

"There's still a lot to work out, I'm sure. Like I say…" he added with faux reassurance, "we'll find a way."

His wife was not convinced. "And we have more medical bills coming in for your rehab and your physio and now we'll have no fucking insurance! Because you are now either fucking dead or unemployed and nobody knows which!"

Mary's voice was now very loud and was causing the dog great concern, so Dover slunk away into the next room. At least this time he wasn't on the end of her wrath for an inappropriate accidental bowel movement or a bit of sick from that disgusting cheap food she fed him.

"We'll sell a car," suggested Laz, "or maybe sell that horse you bought Judith? God knows we could get a fortune for all those video games of Stephen's on E-bay, I should think?"

Mary stood astride his feet as he sat in his chair, hands on her hips, staring down at what she saw as a pathetic little man in an armchair. He'd once had the promise to be a someone, a somebody. But now all he was was a crippled old man, the wrong side of fifty, with no prospects of achieving anything more in his life and she was stuck with him. She should have married Barrington Allison she thought. He was now a hugely successful publisher owning several newspapers and magazines, even if he'd been an obnoxious little creep when she had gone out with him in college. She still seethed anytime she saw some piece of white trash pick up one of his magazines in the supermarket, almost hearing the nickels and quarters they were wasting dropping into his deep, overfull pockets.

"You cannot start selling off our stuff!" Mary stamped her foot. "You cannot! You can't start taking things back from the children just because you have gone and messed things up again!"

"What do you mean again" said Laz "when was the other time"

"Time?" cried Mary "Time? Don't you mean 'times' Lazarus?"

"Like when?" Laz demanded.

"Oh, where to begin? "Like when you invested in banks, what was it 'Lehmann Brothers', because you said 'banks were as safe as houses?"

Laz slowly shrugged.

"Like when the stock market crashed and you sold our portfolio off at the very bottom of the market?"

"Anyone could have done that..." countered Laz.

"Oh, oh, oh" continued Mary "how about when you bought that boat and didn't bother to insure the damn thing? And you and Dick crashed it into the Atlantic City pier and sank the bloody thing the first time you ever went out in it?"

"Um, yes that was unfortunate..." admitted Laz.

"How about the $150,000 you invested in that stupid spinning cooking device that never went anywhere?"

Laz remembered the deep fry spinner with some affection. It was supposed to spin off all the fat from your food after you'd fried it. The public didn't really buy into it though. It seems they like fat and grease in their food.

"I'm sure we'll get a return on that," Laz added, less than enthusiastically. "It'll just take more time.

"In your dreams, Lazarus!" Mary chortled, "your drugs must be kicking in because you are so far removed from reality you don't even see the writing on the wall."

Laz looked at the wall, as indeed the pain killers had in fact kicked in and even though Mary was seriously berating him, a warm glow was gently coursing through his body. There was no writing on the wall that he could see, hard as he looked for it, but the portrait of Mary's father looked down upon him in a most disapproving manner.

"We are going broke Lazarus, right before your eyes. And you have to do something about it... Now!"

Apart from dying again, Laz couldn't really see a way out, even if he could do that he no longer had that YM life insurance policy, he thought. He couldn't afford the firm of lawyers he'd threatened Clarence with, he couldn't even afford a law student come to that. He knew he wouldn't get the life insurance payout for dying and he didn't really, truth be told, want his old job back again. But none of that really bothered him deep down.

What bothered him most was that when he had died, so few people in this world had cared enough about him to come to his final send off. All his life he'd lived thinking he was pleasing people, doing what they wanted, thinking he meant something to them, but no one came. Not even Dick Posman, his best and oldest friend. The thought made a tear come to his eye.

"Oh, don't start blubbering again!" cried Mary marching out of the room. But Lazarus was crying for a totally different reason. He suddenly realized how lonely and alone he now was and it chilled him to his core.

"I shall go and see Dick" he said through his tears to no one in particular.

THE CONFRONTATION

LAZARUS LAID IN wait behind the gothic pillars that made up the grand Market Street facade of the Yours Mutual building in Center City, Philadelphia. He knew Dick's routine by heart. At the end of most days, Dick would be watching the clock, waiting for the little hand to hit six and the big hand to hit twelve. His philosophy was to never leave before six o'clock so he couldn't be accused of shirking his responsibility or not pulling his weight. It didn't make it an unduly long day for him, as he usually never came in before ten each morning, but he liked to still be there when his minions headed home allowing him to slope of to the club after a decent interval, thus giving his staff the impression he might be staying on, working each and every night until the wee hours.

In fact, Dick hated it when anyone else worked even a little bit later than prescribed hours, so much so that he would do the rounds of the Legal department each night about six fifteen, rounding up any stragglers and chivying them along by saying such things as "Hey, Susan? don't you have a home to go to?" or "I wouldn't want to keep that lovely wife of your's waiting, George…" They usually got the message and, even if they had a bundle of work still left undone, it would get shipped home to be completed after dinner or, indeed, in the wee hours.

Dick exited the swirling revolving doors promptly at six thirty five. Laz saw him cut to the left and head towards the club.

"Dick" he yelled emerging from behind the second row of pillars. "It's me! Laz!"

Dick paused for a second mid-step, then continued on, as if not hearing.

"Dick!" Laz cried. "You son-of-a-bitch! Stop! I need to talk to you!" Laz hurried to catch up with him as well as his wounded body would allow.

Dick slowed, turned and opened his arms wide like a mother awaiting her tottering toddler. "Laz, how great to see you! How have you been, I've been meaning to call!"

"Like fuck you have" said Laz arriving in front of his friend. "You never even came to my fucking funeral!"

"Laz, Laz – there's a good reason for that... I was in an accident!"

Lazarus looked unconvinced.

"Let's go to the club and talk about this?" suggested Dick.

Laz shook his head. "No, I don't want to go there, sons of bitches, let's go to Jake's," he suggested referring to a bar just around the corner.

Five minutes later they were seated in a booth, Dick with a triple Chivas on the rocks, Laz with an orange juice and soda.

"Fuck me Laz" said Dick. "An orange juice and soda? What brought this on? You seen the light?"

"The drugs," Laz replied dismissing Dick's concern. "They make me do crazy things if I mix them with the booze..."

"Well, it's still your round!" laughed Dick.

"We'll go Dutch," said Laz.

They eyed each other for a few seconds.

"Christ you look like crap Laz"

"Tell me about it," answered Laz. "Did you hear what 'Yours fucking Mutual' did to me? They shafted me, that's what."

"Yeah, I heard. Clarence told me." Dick struggled with how to finish his thought. "Leanne's doing well though. First quarter sales are up nearly ten points! Dangle is over the moon, I can tell you. He's talking about paying the sales team a bonus for the first time in three years, three years Laz!"

"Yeah, yeah," said Laz. "I heard that."

"And instead of doing the annual conference in the hotel next to fucking Atlantis, Doug is talking... Get this" Dick did a bad impression of a hula dancer seated with a Chivas Regal in front of her. "Can you say Hawaii or even Bora Bora?"

"I'm thrilled for you Dick." Laz responded sarcastically.

"And Leanne's projecting 12% sales growth, year-on-year, for rest of the fiscal," Dick continued.

"Fuck Leanne Dick! Let's talk about me!" Laz shouted. "I'm out of a fucking job, no pay off, no insurance, just 'goodbye Buddy, it's been swell! Good luck with the rest of your life, asshole!'"

"Yeah" agreed Dick. "Bummer."

Dick took a gulp of his whisky, thinking this might well turn into a long one and waved to the waiter to get another one in. The waiter made a squeezing motion and then mimed a soda siphon and Dick looked at Laz's untouched glass and shook his head.

"So what'ya gonna do?" Dick asked Laz.

"Sue the fucks" said Laz without hesitation "Sue you, you fucker!"

Dick patted Lazarus's hand "Now Laz, YM has got deep pockets. Know what I mean? They can take anything you can throw at them and it'll be peanuts to us, them, I mean."

Laz scowled "Well I sure am going to do something. I just maybe haven't figured it out yet."

Dick paused for a second, now aware of the possible conflict of interest he was placing himself in.

"Laz, maybe I should just recluse myself from this conversation? If we're going to court and all?"

Lazarus sighed and waved a hand in Dick's direction.

"No, no, don't leave. I need to talk to you. I want to talk to you." Laz paused for a second. "I have no one anymore that I can talk to," he pleaded.

Over the next fifteen minutes, three Chivas Regals and a club soda with a squeeze of lime, Laz recounted what he knew, and what had been reported to him, of the last few months. Whilst it was pretty fantastic, it didn't include the bit that Dick had heard about Laz actually being inside the incinerator when he woke up and having to bang on the sides of the chamber to alert the operator. But Dick had already noticed the lack of any discernible burn marks earlier at the rehab center.

"The thing is though, Dick." Laz sighed "the thing that gets to me the most is that no one came to the funeral. No one..."

"Not even Mary?" exclaimed Dick.

"Well of course Mary came you idiot, of course my wife showed up – but no one else"

"Not even the kids?"

"Well of course the fucking kids came, you moron. Of course the kids came…"

"Don't get nasty with me Laz," Dick advised, he'd seen Laz fly off the handle more than a couple of times before. "Don't get all mean with me, because if you do, I'll be outta here."

Laz placed his arm on his friend's wrist. "No, no – don't go. What I mean to say is that apart from the family, no one – not even my mother – bothered to show up. Not even you!"

"But I did! I told you," said Dick. "I did show up. I was a bit late mind you, had a meeting with Jennings in accounts about my expenses, but I did show up."

"I saw the video Dick," said Laz, trying to save his friend from any further embarrassment. "I saw the video and you weren't there."

"But Laz, I was there! I swear," protested his friend and former colleague. "I was just pulling into the church when some stupid, bawling black chick, though pretty good looking with a great ass truth be told," he added with a wink "side-swiped me in the parking lot and nearly killed me!"

"A black girl" Laz puzzled. "The one from the service?"

"I don't know Laz. I think she was coming from the service. She looked really upset," Dick told him.

Laz reached inside his jacket pocket and produced the iPhone. "Was it this girl?" he asked, handing the device to

Dick as he pressed 'play'.

THE SHELTER

ARMED WITH THE address that Dick had given him, the one he had exchanged with the girl after the accident in the church parking lot, Laz was headed for downtown Philly. Not the great part of downtown Philadelphia, as in the old part with Carpenter's Hall where the first United States Congress sat for two years, not Liberty Park, not the Art Museum now better known for the Rocky Steps rather than the Cezannes inside; no, he was headed to 63rd and route 30, Lancaster Pike – although they didn't call it that down here. Just thirty, and the town of Lancaster, in Amish Country some thirty miles away, may as well have been on the other side of the world. No one who lived here had ever been there.

Laz slowed his Audi, looking for 16 East 63rd amongst the multitude of cheap clothing stores, ethnic grocers, used car lots selling junkers and the ubiquitous nail and hair extension salons. Parking would not be a problem, he was just worried whether his car would be where he'd left it when he got back.

The GPS found the address. Laz couldn't believe his eyes. He almost wept. It was a homeless shelter. St Jude's Place. He knew from his school days who St Jude was. He was the patron saint of hopeless cases. This couldn't be it. He checked and rechecked the scribbled address that Dick had given him. It matched. He reached for his phone and dialed.

"Dick? It's me Laz."

"Er, Laz?" Dick hesitated. "I'm in a meeting. Can I call you back?"

"No, don't hang up. I just need to check that address you gave me. 16 East 63rd right?"

"Er, yes," said Dick pretending he was checking. "That's it."

"OK"

"Is that Finds?" Laz heard someone say in the background. "You still talk to that dipstick?" Lazarus hung up the connection. Bastards he thought. He got out of the car, locked it, looked around, locked it again. Then he checked the door handles just in case the Audi's security system had suddenly stopped working. With a quick look up and down the street again, nothing and no one looking too suspicious, he turned and headed for the door of the mission.

Laz entered the dingy foyer and was confronted by a tall reception desk behind which sat a very large black man reading the Philadelphia Daily News. He wore a name badge that said 'Welcome to St Jude's – I'm Joshua'. Off to the side, cut off by some kind of half-gate like in a stable, was a long narrow room where perhaps as many as a couple of hundred people were in various stages of eating their lunchtime meal.

"What you want?" said the man. "Lunch? You kinda late,

but I'm sure we can get you sommant."

Laz stammered, more than upset he'd been mistaken for a street person. Christ, he had a $60,000 car outside. He was going to mention that fact, but then thought the better of it. "No, no... though that's very kind. No, I'm not here for lunch," he finally answered.

"You a counsellor?"

"No, I'm..."

"Therapist?"

"No... Er, Joshua?" Laz tried.

"Did I said you could say my name? Did I?"

"Um, no. Sorry," said Laz.

"You a bill collector?" The large man rose getting angry.

"No, no" said Laz getting rather unnerved. "I'm none of those..."

"Then where you at man?"

"I'm looking for someone. This person." Laz held out the piece of paper with the girl's details on it.

"What you want her for?"

"It's personal" said Laz.

"What kind of personal?" asked the large man menacingly.

Laz didn't really know how to answer that so he just leaned in himself and tried to sound menacing too. "Personal kind of personal," he said back and though it came across as rather pathetic, it seemed to do the trick.

"OK, come with me. But if you a bill collector, I'm gonna kick your ass all the way from here to 69th Street."

With that, the man opened the half barn door and led him into the dining hall, past the rows of tables where men and women, young and old, ate their food, some in silence, some in non-stop chatter, some just talking to themselves. Most had clothes that were too large for them or almost in tatters. The smell of humankind hung in the room and mixed with the cabbage soup being served in the kitchen. It was not an odor Laz had ever experienced before nor, he decided, one he wanted to experience again. At the end table, with four or five much older men in their sixties or seventies, sat a pretty thin black girl, with dark hair and blue eyes, eating her soup and dipping her bread in it. The receptionist approached her.

"Tiffany, this man says he has business with you. Personal business... No, sorry. Personal, personal business." Laz nodded.

She looked up from her bowl and eyed him suspiciously.

"What do you want?" she asked him slowly.

"Well, Miss," Laz replied, somewhat nervously, aware now he was now surrounded by a couple of hundred possibly quite hostile people and it suddenly seemed a long way between here and the car, should things not quite go well. "Is there somewhere private we could go?" asked Laz, hopefully.

"No," said the girl.

Laz realized he hadn't really thought this through at all. What was he supposed to say to her? How do you explain this ridiculous mission to a complete stranger?

The large receptionist interjected. "Tell her what you want or I start kicking..."

Laz swallowed. "Well," he said and swallowed again. "My name is Lazarus Finds."

And with that the girl fainted.

THE REVELATION

THEY TOOK THE girl to an office in the back of the building.

A couple of ladies had rushed from the kitchen and overseen the operation. Laz had tried to slip away but had been caught firmly by the scruff of the neck and almost frogmarched along with them. The reaction of all of the diners had been uniform, as one of their own was in need and concern for the girl showed on all their faces. There was distrust, even hate, for the intruder who had brought this upon her.

Laz gave little hope of either him or the Audi emerging from this unscathed. He stood outside the office door guarded by Joshua while the two ladies tended the patient within. Presently they emerged. "You can go in now, Mr Finds," said one.

"What?" said the receptionist. "You gonna let him go in there after that? I'm going in too!"

"No Joshua," said the other lady. "You go back to reception. You know what can happen if you're not on reception."

Joshua thought for a moment remembering just a few of the brawls he had had to break up in only the last week or so. He scowled at Lazarus then opened the door a crack. "I'm going back to reception now, Tiffany. If this jerk tries anything, you just scream and I'll kick his ass all the way from here to 69th Street."

"OK Josh," a quiet, weak voice whispered from within. Laz squeezed between the big man and the door and entered the office closing the door behind him. The girl was sat in an easy chair with a large coffee table in front of her. She motioned for him to sit down opposite.

"I'm sorry about that," he joked trying to clear the air. "It's been a long time since I've had that effect on a woman." Then realizing how stupid and trite that sounded added, "Well, never really."

"No, I'm sorry." she said. "So silly. My bad."

The man and the woman, more a girl really stared at each other for a while, then the girl looked around the room. The silence was awkward for both of them. Laz eventually broke it.

"What happened?" he asked. Then thinking he was being too personal he added, "Not that you have to tell me. I mean it could be private couldn't it? People faint for all kinds of reasons; low blood pressure, iron deficiency, pregnancy. You're not..."

"No.. NO!" the girl responded, horrified.

"I'm sorry! I shouldn't be asking. Only it seemed the thing that made you faint, because you seemed totally fine up until then. It seemed the thing that made you faint..." Laz repeated, "was hearing my name. Lazarus Finds."

He looked at her intensely as if he expected her to faint again and though she didn't, he distinctly saw her flinch.

"See!" he said. "It was that wasn't it? It was my name."

The girl looked up and down, then all around. There was no escape. "It was…" she nodded. "You're that dead guy on the news." Then, "That's so creepy" almost as an afterthought."

"Wow!" said Laz, truly impressed. "You remembered me from the news? But that was months ago."

"Still," said the girl. "TV and all…"

"But why should that make you faint?"

"I don't know?" She shook her head. "I've never met anyone famous before. "It's like if Kanye or Will Smith were to walk in here... I'd probably faint then too."

"I'm hardly Kanye or Will Smith, Tiffany." but Laz secretly glowed a little.

"You're a star, kinda. You were on TV."

"I was on TV because I was nearly mistakenly cremated, not exactly noteworthy in other senses"

"Excuse me," Tiffany eyed him suspiciously, "how did you know my name?"

"I was coming to that," said Laz as he reached into his pocket and pulled out his iPhone. "Do you know what this is Tiffany?" he asked the girl.

"Er, yes, it's an iPhone," she responded. "We do have them in the 'hood too you know?" As an sarcastic addendum she added, "Though most of them is whitie's originally."

"And did you know that iPhones can also make movies?" asked Laz.

Tiffany nodded her head. "Uh-huh. Yes, even us black folk managed to figure out that technology, eventually."

"Watch this," Laz commanded as he pressed play and passed the phone to her. The woman looked at the screen. "So, who is that pretty black girl crying at my funeral?" asked Laz.

The girl looked for a couple of seconds and then passed the phone back. "I have no idea."

He gave her the phone again, "Keep looking, there's lots more to see. You can zoom in on her if you like. Look..."

"Why would I want to do that?"

"Because that's you!"

"No it's not! I've never been there, wherever that is. I don't know what you're talking about!" she shouted at him.

"I think you do. This is my funeral service in Lower Wayne. Now why does a girl like you go all the way up to a church in Lower Wayne for someone she doesn't know?"

"I'm going to call for Joshua."

"Please don't do that, please," a tear started to form in Lazarus's eye.

"Why are you doing this?" the girl asked him bluntly.

"Because I need to know. I had a funeral and nobody came. Only one person cried and it was you and I need to know why." Lazarus wiped his eye. "What's your story Tiffany?"

"What's makes you even think it was me?"

"Well for starters you crashed into my best friend's car as he was arriving at the church. He said you were very upset."

"Maybe I just lost my grandma and needed a place to pray?" offered Tiffany hopefully, a tear forming now in her eye too.

Lazarus thought. "So in the middle of the morning you get in your junker…"

Tiffany looked at him sharply

"Sorry," he continued. "You get in your car. You want to say a prayer for your dear departed grandma. You drive past all these churches, wonderful churches you have in West Philly, you drive to the Main Line where first, driving an '84 Chevy Cavalier will probably get you pulled over anyway…"

The girl shrugged as if she wouldn't know that.

Laz continued "…and second, being black and driving an '84 Chevy Cavalier will almost certainly get you pulled over."

Tiffany nodded as if yes, that much she did know and went back to looking at the iPhone footage.

"Then you get to the church and there's a funeral going on, so instead of turning around or sitting in the back and quietly shedding a few tears for your wonderful grandma, you go sit in the fifth row of someone else's family funeral and cry your eyes out."

Laz looked right at her.

"It doesn't wash Tiffany. There's another explanation."

Tiffany lifted her head up from the tiny screen and looked Lazarus in the eye.

"OK, try this one," she advised him. "I'm your daughter."

Lazarus Finds fainted.

THE EXPLANATION

JOSHUA WAS TAPPING Laz's cheek as he passed a bottle of smelling salts under his nose. "Man, you two are a fine pair," he said, "I ain't never seen nothing like this before."

Everything was blurry in front of Laz, he could just about see five or six faces, all black, staring down at him. Was he dead? Were all the angels black?

"Am I dead again?" he whispered to no one in particular.

"No, you ain't dead Man, you's just participating in National Fainting Week." Joshua laughed. "Reckon it's my turn next. Anyone behind me better run for cover!"

Laz shook his head and pushed the smelling salts away. "I'm OK, I'm OK, " he assured the throng.

"Can we be alone again everyone" asked Tiffany "please?"

"Are you sure honey?" asked one of the ladies in the background.

Joshua started to wobble. "I don't know, I think I'm going down..."

A voice at the back snapped. "Joshua! Reception Desk, now!"

"OK, but I could kill someone if I fall down out there..."

"I'll kill you sugar, if you don't go!" assured the voice.

One by one they left the room and Tiffany closed the door behind them. Then she started to aimlessly wander around the office for what seemed rather a long time. The silence was deafening. Laz eventual whispered but it seemed like a shout.

"Did you say what I thought you said?"

"How much do you remember?"

"To the bit about you being my daughter, was there more?"

"No, that was pretty much it," confirmed Tiffany.

"How do you know?" asked Laz.

"Well, let's put it this way," said Tiffany. "You were my 21st birthday present."

Lazarus looked at her quizzically, shaking his head to try and clear the fog. "I don't understand."

"Well, I grew up in the Northern Liberties without a daddy," the girl explained. "It wasn't quite the up-and-coming place it is now. Back in the day, there was a lot of us girls without daddies, but not so many of us coffee colored ones. It's tough being half-black half-white, you don't know what you are. Some of the black boys want you because they look at you like a piece of white tail..."

Laz raised his eye brows and opened his eyes wider.

"Sorry," the girl continued, "I don't mean to shock you. But growing up down there ain't pretty."

"Sorry," said Laz. "Please carry on…"

She did. "Anyhow, then they treat you like trash because you isn't all black. The black girls will beat the shit out of you for that, and they'll never accept you for one of them. At school, you have to hope they let you sit at the black kids lunch table in the school cafeteria, because you know if you sit at the white kids table you can never go back. So you sit on your own."

"And all that led you here?" supposed Laz.

"In a roundabout way, I suppose it did," she agreed.

Laz shook his head. "So what was this about your birthday?'

"So I would always be asking my Momma who you were."

"Me?" asked Laz.

"As in my father," she clarified. "I wanted to find out because I had this hope, this crazy dream really. that we could move away from there and be near you and I could go to a white kids school and I could pretend to be like Halle Berry or Mariah Carey."

"And she told you?" suggested Laz.

"Hell no!" Tiffany cried. "She would never tell me." She sniffed and Laz passed her his handkerchief.

"So how did you come to think that you were?" Laz asked her. "My daughter, I mean," still unconvinced and now slowly recovering from the shock.

"And so for my 21st birthday my Momma said to me, she said 'Angel, for your birthday you can have whatever you want. You just name it and if I can afford it you can have it' and I said 'Momma, there's only one thing that I want and this won't cost you a dime...' and do you know what she said?"

"No?" said Laz.

"That's right" said Tiffany "that's exactly what she said. 'No!' I didn't even have to tell her what I wanted. She knew. I said 'Momma, I'm twenty one years old, I deserve to know who he is. I promise I wont bug him, I won't approach him, I just need to know who my father is...'"

"And she told you?" Laz asked.

"Oh not until there was a whole lot of tears shed and screaming done, we do that a lot in our family by the way, 'cause she does not want her life changed. She is happy just how she is and don't want that spoiled. She did this this for me, so I would know and I promised her I would never approach you"

"And how did you find me?"

"Yeah, sure thing it was hard, 'cause Lazarus Finds is such an everyday, common name isn't it?" she half laughed and half sniffed through the handkerchief. "The phone book is just full of them. Why my street had three on it alone!"

Laz smiled. "Yes, I suppose you hardly need to be a detective do you?"

"I looked up where you lived, where you worked. I used to see you coming and going. I used to stand next to you in the hot dog line. Standing next to my daddy getting our lunch. Sometimes I'd take the R5 out to Wynnewood, sit in your carriage, get off at your stop, then make my way back to Centre City. Once, I sat next to you and watched you as you did your work on the train. My daddy, important man, doing the business. Other times I went by myself. I saw your house. I saw your fancy wife in her Mercedes, the little kids in the back, my half brother and sister who I ain't never gonna be able to talk to." She wiped her eyes again.

Lazarus's jaw had dropped and his eyes were opened wider than even before. "You followed me?" he gasped.

"Sure thing, I was a regular little stalker," said Tiffany,. "For a few months anyway, but it was eating me up inside not being able to approach you or them and I couldn't take it anymore. So I stopped. I had to stop and I vowed I'd never do it again."

"When was that?" asked Laz.

"Oh, about five years ago or so," said Tiffany.

"I see," said Laz thinking back and wondering if he recalled anyone lurking outside the house or at the office behind those same pillars he had hidden behind when he was stalking Dick.

"And then when I read that you had died, I thought I really needed to be at the funeral to say goodbye. I wanted Momma to come, but she wouldn't."

"She lives here then?"

"By the way," asked the girl. "You do remember who my mother is, don't you, or did you have a thing for black chicks back then?"

"Oh no," smiled Laz. "I remember. I remember her very well."

"Tell me her name then," said the girl.

"What?" said Laz.

"If you're telling the truth and you weren't just running around with every hot black college chick," she smiled sweetly at him, "coz you know there's some white boys what do that, you can tell me her name."

Laz thought that he'd already taken a lot of what this Tiffany person had told him on trust already, in reality she could be anybody. In reality this could just be a scam. "How about you tell me her name?" he asked her,. "Make sure we're all on the same page here."

The two looked at each other like gunfighters in an old Western before the girl spoke. "Well this is getting us nowhere fast'," she said. Reaching onto the desk she took two pens and a stack of post-it pads. Tearing the pad in half, she gave one half to Laz and a pen. "Here," she said. "You write down your name and I'll write down my name…"

Laz took the pen and yellow pad. "It's a bit like 'Final Jeopardy' he half-joked, recalling one of Mary's favorite game shows. The girl didn't react, but wrote on her yellow pad instead.

They both wrote on their pads and held them face down. "You go first" she instructed him.

Laz turned over his pad, it read *Roberta*.

"Now your turn," he told her.

Tiffany turned over her pad, it read *Jocelyn*. Laz thought he should have been relieved, but his heart sank.

The girl then pulled off the top sheet of the yellow post-it, it now read *aka Jocelyn Roberta Myers*. "She always hated Jocelyn," she said and laughed. "But who knew with her being at a fancy college and all, who knew what she would call herself?"

"It was Roberta," confirmed Laz, sniffing and holding back the tears and all the memories that suddenly flooded back to him.

"I guess it was" whispered Tiffany. "What was she like
back then?"

Laz sniffed, took the handkerchief back and wiped his eyes.
"She was exquisite. She was extraordinarily beautiful,
funny and so bright. The smartest girl, no person," he
corrected himself. "The smartest person I'd ever met."

The girl nodded and smiled.

"Did you know her long?" she asked.

"Just a few weeks, maybe just two, three months I think?"
said Laz. "And then she just disappeared."

Tiffany looked down into her lap. "They sent her away.
She was pregnant... With me. They sent her to my great-
grandma's in Mississippi. She finished her degree in the
end, but not at Villanova, at Ole Miss. It took her six
years."

"Oh my God." Laz shook his head. "I should have known
she wouldn't leave me. I should have looked harder!"

Tiffany reached out to him and touched his hand. "It's OK,
you were just kids. Everything worked out. She's happy.
She's fine now," the girl assured him.

Lazarus clambered to his feet as best he could.

"I really must see her!" He reached for Tiffany with both

hands. "You must take me to her!"

"No!" Tiffany shouted. "I knew this would happen. She knew this would happen. No, no way!"

"You must, you must! Please - or I will follow you…" Laz threatened. "I will stalk you for a change!"

"No don't," cried the girl now sobbing. "I promised her!"

"I will find her. I must find her!" shouted Laz. "Don't you understand? This was all meant to be!"

"Leave her be" cried Tiffany. "Please leave her be. She's finally happy!"

"No" shouted Laz to the sound of several sets of footsteps racing down the corridor. "I will follow you day and night until I find her. I need to put this right! I will put this right!"

The door flew open and Laz found himself lifted off his feet as a voice rang in his ear. "Didn't I tell you enough times, Buddy? I am now going to kick your ass from here to 69th Street. Get the hell outta here and don't come back!"

Lazarus sensed it might be Joshua.

THE LAWYER

LAZARUS WAS SITTING in one of the somewhat less salubrious of the many meeting rooms of Pinkerton, Pinkerton, Pinkerton, Smythe. They had been his lawyers for years and Mary's family's legal representatives for generations before that. P,P,P & S had existed here in Philadelphia, in one form or another, well back into the early 19th century. The many visages of esteemed legal personages staring down upon Laz and the vast array of legal tomes lined up along the library shelves whispered to him, "If anyone can screw those bastards Sir, we can!" Though much more politely, of course.

Laz waited for what seemed an age. It used to be when he arrived for an appointment he would be met promptly, but since the word of his 'demise' had gotten out, his importance seemed to have waned. His meeting was scheduled for four and it was a quarter past already. Usually Tom Pinkerton would have offered him a scotch by now. Presently the door opened and a much younger man than Laz had expected walked in. He barely made eye contact with his client.

"Good afternoon Mr Finds," he said matter-of-factly. "My name is Scott Breslin, glad you've made yourself comfortable." As if sitting down for twenty minutes waiting for my appointment was a crime, thought Laz.

"'I'm here to talk to you about your issues with your

previous employer, Yours Mutual."

"Where's Tom?" asked Laz.

"I'm sorry?" replied the young lawyer who seemed just a year or two out of Villanova or Penn.

"My lawyer, Tom Pinkerton," clarified Laz.

"Well, he's with a client right now Mr Finds," the kid advised.

"I'm his client," exclaimed Laz. "I've been his fucking client for 25 years!"

"Listen Mr Finds," the newly-minted lawyer continued through gritted teeth. "You can wait to get an appointment with Tom Pinkerton and he'll charge you $2,500 for the same advice that I'm going to charge you 250 bucks for. He may even advise you to do something that's going to cost you a whole lot more money, money that I don't think you have right now. So, without being impolite, I suggest you sit down and listen to me for five minutes. OK?"

Laz was stunned. No one had spoken to him like that since, well since Judith said she wanted that new horse last Christmas, but this guy was even more effective.

"OK," said Laz guardedly.

"Here's the deal," Scott continued. "First of all, I think you've been treated abominably. I followed your story. Pretty remarkable, almost being cremated. Something like that is enough to put many people into the nuthouse."

"I suppose..."

"How do you feel about it?"

"Well, in some ways I actually feel better. Of course, I have no job, no income and huge expenses which is why I'm here" Laz added.

"And we have no hope of winning." concluded Breslin.

Laz was stunned. "For this you are going to charge me $250?"

"In court," the lawyer added.

Scott Breslin stared at Laz. "Let's go back. You 'die'. As soon as the death certificate is issued, your wife sends it to your employers."

"Took it…" interrupted Laz.

"What's that?" said the lawyer.

"She took it into them," advised Lazarus. "The ink was still wet on it I believe. You can see a smudge if you look closely. She hand-delivered it."

"Boy, she was keen!" Breslin observed.

"Twenty million dollars of insurance money can be quite the motivator," Laz agreed.

"Anyhow," the lawyer continued. "She, your wife, takes the death certificate to your employer. who also happen to be your life insurer. in order to claim on your life insurance. First they terminate your employment, because you're dead and then they immediately promote your deputy and give her a handsome raise and a new contract. That's OK within in law, understand? We can't change that."

Laz nodded.

The lawyer continued. "Then they start to process your life insurance pay out, that takes a few days longer, various boxes have to be ticked and checked. However, before they finish, suddenly you're not dead. You're alive after all, so the claims department of your company don't have to pay out. You understand that, yes?"

"Yes, yes," said Laz exasperated. "I knew all that already. Tell me something I don't know!"

"Alright, how about this one? Did you know the company's HMO don't even have to pay your insurance bills because you were no longer an employee when you 'woke up' and hadn't registered for COBRA yet or since, but I wouldn't mention that to them if I were you, it could get very expensive."

"So what do we do?" Laz gasped.

"You say you want to sue Yours Mutual?" the lawyer questioned.

"Uh huh..." his nod getting weaker, less and less convincing with each.

The young lawyer continued. "You could do that, but they are a very large firm with an excellent legal team. Such litigation could take years, cost hundreds of thousands of dollars. Best possible scenario, perhaps a five per cent chance you win."

Laz brightened. "Five percent's not bad, is it?"

The lawyer continued. "Five percent is terrible! Even then, you get your job back and they pay your costs. But we know they don't want you working there already don't we? So a year down the line, they lay you off or even fire you and you're back where you are today."

"They could do that?" gasped Laz.

"Sure!" he replied. "And they may not even be required to pay your costs. Worst case scenario, you lose, you pay my costs and their costs – hundreds, perhaps, millions of dollars."

"Millions?" echoed Laz. "Millions?

"Could be. Is your house in both you and your wife's names?"

"Yes..." Laz answered weakly, unsure whether this would be a good or a bad thing.

"Good, then they can't touch that. You'd just have to pay it all yourself and your wife could keep the house," smiled the lawyer.

"Why does that somehow not reassure me?" asked Lazarus.

The two men looked at each other for a few moments. Laz looked at the portraits of the great men hanging on the walls around him, hoping somehow for inspiration. Nothing came, they all seemed shrouded in doom and gloom anyhow.

"Here's what we do," Breslin said brightly. "We write them a letter!"

"A letter?" said Laz. "How will a letter help?"

"Letters are great!" said the young Villanova grad. "Corporations love litigation, it's what they do. They have whole teams and departments set up for that. They revel in all that stuff. It makes them feel very important and justifies the existence of their entire legal budget."

"So?" asked Laz, confused.

"But," advised the whiz-kid lawyer, "a really great letter scares the shit out of them!"

THE ADMISSION

IT WAS AFTER dinner and they had just played Jeopardy, an evening ritual that had begun when they first were married. Now Laz was preparing to play his own version of the game with Mary, only she could not possibly hope to guess the answer and the value of the stakes were so much higher. Mary was now intensely watching Wheel of Fortune, but Laz could only see the 'bankrupt' key go round and round and wonder whether the wheel would stop there for him every time if he ever got on the show.

She was yelling at the television.

"Take a 'K', take a 'K' you idiot!"

"I'll have a 'T' please Mark," said the voice from the TV.

"There's no 'T'," said Mark.

"Of course there's no 'T' you dimwit. The answer's 'COFFEE BREAK'. Where's the 'T' in coffee break?"

"Susie, spin the wheel," commanded Mark. "Eight hundred."

"I'll have an 'L', Mark"

"There's no 'L'."

"Jesus wept!" cried Mary.

"You should go on this show," suggested Laz. "You're very good..." He continued, hoping a little flattery might help his own little game show to come.

"They're a bunch of brainless nincompoops. I think they pick them by their bra size."

Lazarus shifted nervously in his seat. "Mary, when this is over, there's something I need to talk to you about."

"Good news?" she enquired. "Is it good news? God, I could use some good news."

"Well..." Laz kind of half-smiled and half-nodded implying there was that possibility. "Some might think that it was. In a way, sort of. I suppose."

"Oh God, then tell me now," she demanded flicking the TV off and throwing the remote down onto the couch beside her. "Is it the money, did you get the money? Did they pay out the life insurance?" She held her hands together as if in a prayer, though the last time she had been in a church was for Laz's funeral.

"No, then didn't pay the life insurance."

"The death benefit then?"

"No, not the death benefit either," said Laz irritated the conversation had immediately gone down the money path.

"They gave you your job back," she said crossing herself. "Well, that's better than nothing I suppose. It'll get you out of the house at least!"

"Mary, it's nothing like that, none of those things!" Lazarus hissed.

"Then what the hell is it Laz?" she shouted. "Get to the fucking point!"

"It's a long story," he sighed, let me get you a drink. He poured her Scotch.

"Have one yourself," she said. "You look like you need it."

"No I'll stick with the club soda, thanks."

"You're still off the booze, I can't say I believe it." Mary raised her her glass to him. "Cheers. Now, get a move on, Modern Family is on in four minutes."

Laz laughed as he considered the irony of the channel line-up that night. "Well…" he started nervously, "When I was at university, Villanova not Widener, before I met you…" he laughed. "Oh long, long, long before I met you."

"Yes" interjected Mary impatiently.

"I had a relationship with a woman."

"A prof?" Mary gasped.

"No!" said Laz shocked. "A girl, a fellow student, a biology student..."

"Really?" Mary winked. "Biology eh, so she knew when all the bits were and how everything worked then, I suppose?"

"Please don't make this seedy Mary," asked Lazarus. It's difficult enough as it is."

"Go on then," advised his wife.

"Anyway, she was black."

"Even more interesting," added Mary. "I didn't know you went for that sort of thing, but I can't say I haven't been there."

"Really?" Laz was shocked. "Mary, please!"

"Another time Lazarus, this is your moment." Mary gave him a wave with her hand. "Continue. I'm cool... I'm chillin' man! Ice cold..."

"And can we cut the phony street talk please?" requested Laz. "I'm trying to be serious here."

"Sure thing bro," advised Mary.

"Anyway, it has come to light, in the last few days, that this girl and I made a," Laz took a deep breath. "That this girl and I... made a..."

"Made a what?" asked Mary.

"Um, we made a, um..."

"What? You've got thirty-two seconds before Modern Family starts so get a move on," Mary advised.

"A baby!" Laz trembled as the words finally exited his mouth.

Mary's screams echoed around the house bringing the children running down the stairs, Lazarus had never seen them move so fast before. They never came when he called them. Dover was barking furiously and jumping up at Laz.

"What?" screamed Mary. "You fathered a bastard black baby! Sweet Jesus, Mary and Joseph!"

Where is all this religion coming from, wondered Lazarus?

"Children, your father has gone and got a black whore pregnant and got himself a black bastard baby!" screamed their mother.

Judith screamed and started to cry and Stephen just stood there and said "Ewweh."

"Mary," pleaded Laz. "Please tell them the truth. This was twenty six years ago, it's not like it was yesterday!"

"IT'S THE SAME THING DADDY!" shouted Judith.

"She's a lovely girl, you'd like her." Laz tried to work the room. "Her name is Tiffany."

He looked for any sign of interest in their new step-sister. "She's fallen on hard times and we need to help her..."

"Help her?" cried Mary. "Are you out of your mind! Why should we try and help her and your bastard black baby?"

"She's not a baby any more!" defended Laz. "She's a grown woman, but she's had a difficult life growing up in the ghetto and she's ended up on the streets..."

"Oh my God!" screamed Judith. "She's a hooker!"

"Will someone shut that dog up!" cried Laz, as Dover ran barking in circles around them.

"Cool," said Stephen. "I've got a sister who's a hooker..."

"She's not a hooker" shouted Laz. "She lives in a hostel. She's quite respectable. She just needs a little financial help to give her a lift."

"Money?" Mary's eyes grew wide. "You're suggesting giving away what's left of our children's inheritance to your bastard, black daughter hooker, are you?"

And with that, Judith picked up his walking stick and hit him hard over the head. The last thing he remembered was someone saying, "You're not selling my fucking pony!"

THE LAST STRAW

"IT'S OVER LAZ," said Mary as she dabbed at the deep wound above his left eye. "You know, you might want to pop down to the hospital with this."

"Do you think so?" asked Laz, pleased she was showing him at least a little concern and civility.

They sat in the bathroom of his beautiful Main Line home, the one that he had worked twenty five years to procure, pay off and maintain. It was beautiful from the outside, a lovely lawn, sweeping driveway, fake doric pillars to welcome its occupants and visitors, five bedrooms with three en-suites, a pool, sauna and jacuzzi. Just paying for it had almost wiped him out and now, as he sat in the white marble tiled bathroom, he couldn't remember one happy moment that he had spent in it.

"I think it's been over for a long time Laz," she continued. "I think we were just staying together for the children."

"I wasn't!" protested Laz.

"Weren't you?" said Mary.

"No" said Laz. He thought for a moment, "I think I was just staying together."

"How do you mean?" he didn't now whether she sounded

puzzled or annoyed.

"I think" he continued, "I think I just couldn't think of anything else to do."

"Exactly" said Mary "you've made my point."

Laz screamed "Owwww."

"Oh, that was the iodine. That might hurt a bit... Sorry" Mary added.

"Probably best you didn't tell me," offered Lazarus in compensation.

"I'm sorry I hit you Laz," Mary apologized. "I shouldn't have done that."

"I don't think you did hit me"

"Of course I did!."

Laz was confused. "I distinctly remember Judith..."

"Laz! Judith would never..." Mary's eyes grew wide, "your own daughter! How dare you even suggest it!"

"But..." protested Laz.

"No, it was me," admitted Mary. "I picked up your stick and hit you good and hard I'm afraid. I don't know what came over me."

"Mary?" Laz tried to sound conciliatory. "What if we saw a therapist? Maybe we could work things out? Start again. We used to be happy, didn't we?"

Mary started applying a dressing to his head and he could see in her reflection in the mirror that she genuinely seemed to be trying to remember.

"You know Laz?" she said. "I really can't remember a time when we ever were, can you?"

"When we first got married?" Laz suggested.

Mary stared vacantly into the distance. "Well, I was happy to be getting married, I suppose. All my friends were either married or getting married and I'd already been engaged twice before and they didn't work out."

"Third time lucky then, I suppose?" suggested Laz.

"Best of a bad lot," mused Mary out loud. "It wasn't really a great year, but you did have good prospects Laz, you just seemed to get stuck."

Lazarus felt rather insulted. "I think I did OK! Senior Vice President of a major insurance firm, house on the Main Line."

"Oh come on Laz," smiled Mary. "It's Yours Mutual, not the Pru..."

"It's still a good job!"

"Which you don't have any more if you haven't noticed" snapped Mary.

"Oh let's not start again," pleaded Laz. "I thought we just got past that."

"Yes, alright Laz," Mary calmed a little. "Anyway I've given this a little thought and I've come up with a plan."

"A plan?" echoed Laz.

"Yes, a plan," said Mary trying to hide her excitement. "You see I do plan things and I'm prepared to take responsibility for my own life now, mine and the children's – if you'll agree."

"Go on" said Lazarus, curious now but sceptical.

"Well," Mary continued, eyes flashing, now excited. "I figured out that if you hand the house over to me, as well as three quarters of the remaining investments and half of what's in the bank accounts, then we – the children and I - will be able to manage just fine on our own and you'll be able to start a new life!"

Lazarus couldn't understand how his wife, Mary, who had never attempted to balance a checkbook, who had never opened a bank statement, never looked at a credit card summary or an invoice from a contractor could possibly have done this.

"But how could you possibly know this" he shook his head "you have no idea what it even takes to run this house, what the school fees are, what's in the portfolio, what's even in the bank. I can't let you do this."

Mary looked concerned, she thought this would be easy.

"Lazarus, you should sleep on the couch downstairs tonight. I don't want you taking another tumble. Let's go down"

She helped him to his feet, guided him through the door, along the landing and down the sweeping staircase that had so nearly taken his life some five months previously. As she walked she explained.

"I had a financial advisor, a friend, take me through the books Laz," she told him. "It's all doable. He will oversee all my money and keep me in check. Probably better than you did I expect," she laughed.

"It's much too soon Mary," he protested.

"Oh, I've been thinking about this for a long time Laz," she told him as she guided him down the stairs, noticing as they went that the CSI people still hadn't quite got all of the chalk marks out of the slate and making a mental note to give them another call in the morning. "If anything your little tumble down *les escaliers* just prolonged the whole process." She sighed and added, "As well as seriously depleting the accounts."

"I'm not sure, Mary," he protested vainly.

"It's all for the best Lazarus," the wife insisted.

"Who is this financial advisor?" Laz demanded, overly emphasizing the final couple of words.

"No one you know." she lied "No one you know."

As she tucked him up on the couch and placed a pillow behind his head she reminded him. "You know this is for the best Laz, this has been coming for a long time." Secretly, although he hated to admit it, he knew she was right, and secretly he was relieved the moment had finally arrived and it was she who initiated it, but still...

Mary switched out the light and leaned over him to give him a kiss, thought better of it and gently tapped his shoulder twice instead. He winced. It was the bad shoulder, but she didn't notice in the dark.

"Probably best if you move out in the morning Laz, OK?" he heard as she drifted out of the room.

He grunted.

He tried to sleep, but couldn't, all these thoughts were tumbling through his head; Tiffany, the lawyer, the hostel, Mary and the children. Fifteen minutes or so later he heard her open the living room door again and then heard her soft footsteps walking towards him. Could she have had a change of heart he wondered? He opened his eyes and saw a figure silhouetted against the moonlight, leaning over him.

"You're not going to sell my fucking pony!" the voice

hissed.

THE TRUTH

DICK THOUGHT IT was wise to meet a little ways away from Yours Mutual and had suggested Morning Glory, a quaint cafe located in the Italian Market area of South Philly.

Laz had loved the Italian market from when he was a boy. Often on Saturdays he would still wander down 9th Street from Christian, have the now 90 year old Vic cut him a pork loin, roll it in that special Canulli's spice mix and strap on some crackling - just the way he had done since Laz was a kid. Or he'd go into DiBruno's, determined to only eat some free samples, not to buy anything mind, and leave half an hour later with fifty bucks worth of the most amazing cheeses, salamis and breads. Sometimes he'd slip into Fante's, look at all the great espresso and pasta machines and find himself buying a little kitchen gadget that, just in the moment suddenly seemed essential, but in the back of his mind he knew he would never use, nor probably not remember what it was for by the time he got home. But that's what the Italian Market was about. It was an experience, an original Philly experience.

Dick was in his business suit, ready to head off to the YM on Market a few blocks to the north, but a world away from Little Italy. Laz was relaxed in shorts, tee shirt and Phillies baseball cap. It was a lovely breezy summer's day, the hot stifling Philly heat had yet to arrive this year.

"How so?" Dick looked at his friend quizzically.

"I kinda caused a scene," confessed Laz.

"You?" laughed Dick. "Cause a scene? Now there's a first! What did you do this time?"

"Dick," Laz whispered confidentially, "there's something you should know about Tiffany."

Dick leaned in. "Tell all, good buddy."

Laz looked across to the table alongside and measured his tone and voice level to ensure the woman could not hear. "Tiffany's kind of fallen on hard times. She doesn't exactly live on the street but she lives in or around a hostel shelter thing down on East 63rd."

"No shit." Dick looked genuinely sympathetic, "that's rough. Rough place too. Bad scene."

"I want to try and help her" said Laz.

"So you tried to kidnap her?" suggested Dick.

"No" Laz protested. "Where is that food? I went a bit over the top demanding to see her mother, and now I don't think she'll want to see me again"

Dick laughed as the waitress approached the table with their plates, setting them down in front of them. "Oh, I think she will..." He advised.

"How's that?" enquired Laz.

Dick looked him in the eye. "Listen, she's on the street, in a shelter, whatever. You go down there with an envelope full of money she'll see you alright. And you know what?"

Laz scowled at his friend hoping he wasn't right but thinking he probably was.

"What?" Laz answered him.

"She'll keep seeing you."

Dick started hungrily tucking into his rib-eye steak and two eggs. "So how did Mary take it" he asked though a mouthful of cow.

"Not well," Laz replied removing his Phillies cap.

"Holy crap!" cried Dick. "What the fuck happened to your head?"

"DO YOU MIND?" yelled the lady at the next table. "I have young children here!"

"I'm so sorry Ma'am!" Dick apologized pointing to his friend's head, "but have you seen this?"

Laz relayed the whole story to Dick, watching his language as he did, avoiding the displeasure of the angry woman at the next table. He ended the tale with him sleeping on the couch but left out the visit by Judith in the night.

"So she threw you out, huh?" Dick asked through his chewing.

"It was a mutual decision," corrected Laz as he pondered his tofu scrambler and wondered whether he had made the right decision. "I'll be staying at the Radnor Motel, until I get a permanent place, probably spend all day watching Oprah."

"Sounds like you should be staying with Timpani," Dick laughed.

"It's Tiffany!" Laz corrected for the third time, now he was sure Dick was doing it on purpose.

"So why did she whack you, was it about the kid?" he snorted.

"I walked into..."

"I know, 'a door'" finished Dick. "So what's the deal? Trial separation? Cooling down period? Might not be a bad idea. When you think of it this whole thing must have been pretty stressful on her as well."

Laz shook his head as he twirled a piece of soggy tofu in front of his eyes. "She says it's over Dick. Finished! Kaput! Finito! No Mas!"

"No way!" Dick sounded shocked, almost too shocked.

"And do you know what?" said Laz. "She had it all

worked out."

"Really?" replied Dick, too quizzically.

"She gave me a piece of paper where she had gone over all the assets, the house value, all the accounts, the entire portfolio valued up to the close of the market yesterday." Laz shook his head, "it was remarkable."

"That is remarkable" replied the lawyer, too impressed. Dick nervously cut a too big a bit of ribeye and shoved it in his mouth and chewed.

"She said she had 'a friend' help her do it," sneered Laz. "I wonder what kind of 'friend' that was? One that balances more than her checkbook I'll bet!"

"Oh, you don't think she'd do something like that do you Laz?" Dick mumbled through the steak. "Not after what you've been through."

Laz gave up on the tofu, stopping drinking was one thing, trying to eating healthily was something quite different altogether. He should have had the breakfast burrito with the red peppers and chile sauce. Was it too late to still get it he wondered?

"Honestly Dick," he mused, "I wouldn't blame her. I've not been the greatest husband, not by a long shot. God knows most weeknights I'm getting pissed at the club with you, most weekends I'm on the golf course with you or getting pissed again in the 19th hole." He shook his head and said in an exasperated tone, "but I thought that was how she wanted it."

"I don't know," said Dick. "Women! I've never understood them. That's why I've never got married, never will. Have a bit on the side every now and again, as soon as they start getting touchy-feely, I'm off like a bat-out-of-hell. It does rather limit the number of social occasions I can go to these days though. There's always one or two of them there..."

"Anyway, she wants the house, lock, stock and smoking barrel. She wants half of what's in the joint accounts. She wants seventy five percent of the portfolio, which would have been a lot more four years ago before that moron Peter what-his-name lost half of it" explained Laz. "And that's it. Nothing more. No maintenance. Nothing"

""Nothing?" exclaimed Dick.

Laz shook his head, he would get a couple of eggs he thought after Dick left, "Nothing! I think she's given me up as a lost cause. She says I can make a new start on the cash and good luck to me."

"Still, can she manage on that?" Dick asked.

"Well," said Laz, "her 'friend' seems to think so, but maybe I should go over the numbers with her one more time?"

Dick shook his head. "I shouldn't worry, Aubrey's very thorough."

"True," said Laz

For quite a few moments no one said anything, while they both mulled over what had just been said. Dick hoping Laz hadn't actually heard what he said. Laz wondering whether he had actually heard what Dick had said correctly. As each man went from believing one thing then the other and then back again time seemed to stand still.

"'Aubrey?'" said Laz "you said 'Aubrey.'"

"What?"

"You said 'Aubrey's very thorough'"

The two men stared at each other, Dick's mouth started to open and close very slowly but no words came. His lawyer's mind raced for a response. It was like being back in court, desperately seeking a response in cross examination. Suddenly he had it.

"But you said, Aubrey's helping her with her accounts" said Dick, with an almost audible 'phew'.

"No I didn't," responded Laz. "I said a friend is helping her with her accounts."

"Ah!" said Dick triumphantly. "Well there you have it!"

"Have what?" cried Laz.

"You see," said Dick advisedly, "it's the way you pronounce 'f-r-i-e-n-d'. It comes out sounding almost like 'Aubrey', not quite I'll admit, but with the noise in here and those kids squawking over there and everything, it does rather."

Dick was beginning to think he'd gotten away with this and was feeling rather proud, in fact he almost believed it himself. Laz looked at Dick in bewilderment. Dick started to hurriedly finish his breakfast.

"They sound as much alike as apple and orange!" he told him. "Why would you bring Aubrey into the discussion, unless you knew he was doing this? What do you know Dick?"

Dick shook his head. "Laz, I misspoke. I know nothing!"

Laz stopped Dick's hand from raising the coffee cup and finishing the dregs. There would be no quick getaway this day. "So a moment ago you misheard, and now you misspoke. What do you know Dick? Best friend?"

"Like I said, nothing Laz." Dick stared hard at Laz with his courtroom face, though he hadn't practiced it for a while.

"Is that bastard Aubrey screwing my wife?"

"Of course not!" Dick laughed.

Laz tightened his grip on Dick's hand.

"Is he?" he repeated much louder, with a threat of violence in his voice.

"Let go Laz!" Dick tried to calm him. "You're causing a scene."

"Dick, you fucking tell me or I'll pour this hot coffee all over your fucking suit," Laz hissed.

Dick thought about his upcoming review with Dangle in ten minutes and seemed to deflate before Laz's eyes. He released the coffee cup and slumped back in his chair.

"Yes," he admitted weakly.

Laz gave a sardonic half laugh. "How long"

"Two years or so?"

"Two fucking years, two fucking years and you, my best friend never thought to tell me about it?"

"I didn't want you to get hurt Laz," Dick pleaded. "Did you think I enjoyed being at the club with you while Aubrey was, well, you know."

Laz's eye's shot open wide and his jaw dropped. He almost shouted. "You mean all those nights when I was at the club alone with you and that S.O.B. would leave early, he was banging my wife?"

A child at the next table started crying and the waitress came over and told them to settle down or leave.

"You're supposed to be my best friend Dick," Lazarus hissed. "And you were fucking me as much as Aubrey was fucking Mary"

"Laz," Dick protested. "It wasn't like that"

"And did you call him every night when I was leaving so he could get his prick out in time?"

Dick just stared back at Laz. There was nothing to say.

"Get out, Dick!" advised Laz. "I never want to see you again." Laz turned and looked out the window.

"Laz, please?" Dick went to place his hand on Laz's shoulder but Laz just pushed him away. The lawyer stood up and looked down at him.

"You had it coming Laz. You abandoned them a long time ago." Dick turned away and headed out the door and north towards Market Street.

Bastard never even paid for his breakfast, thought Laz.

THE LETTER

PINKERTON, PINKERTON, PINKERTON, SMYTHE
1401 MARKET STREET
SUITE 1000
PHILADELPHIA
PA 19001

Mr Douglas R. Dangle III
Yours Mutual Insurers Inc.
1501 Chestnut Street
Suite 1650
Philadelphia
PA 19002

15th July 201_

Dear Doug

Re: Lazarus S. Finds

I write on behalf of our client, Mr Finds, in the hope of finding a course (other that litigation) in determining the continuance or agreeable termination of his contracts with you, in a manner that is fair and equitable to all parties.

Whereas, the course of events that led our client to be in the situation he is in today is well known, it is worth briefly restating them for the record.

1. On the night of December 3rd last, Mr Finds suffered a terrible fall at his home in Lower Wayne after spending the evening at his club with your chief counsel Mr Richard L. Posman. He was pronounced dead at the scene by paramedics, this was later confirmed at Benjamin Franklin hospital. His body was transferred the next morning to Piscini's undertakers where Mr Finds' wife Mary determined not to have the body embalmed and had it held there for the funeral on December 6th.

2. You received from Mary Finds a death certificate on December 4th and thus terminated his employment and replaced him immediately and, without any job search for a better external candidate, with his deputy. At the same time Mrs Finds filed a claim for payment under Mr Find's life insurance policy which was also held by your company.

3. Mr Finds' funeral was held, as planned, on December 6th and, while not a mandatory requirement, it did not go

unnoticed that there was not a single member of the Yours Mutual senior team in attendance. However, once Mr Finds' coffin was removed to the crematorium the attendant there noticed a dull knock-knock-knock and muffled groaning emanating from within the casket. It was then it was discovered Mr Finds was still alive.

4. Mr Finds was then subject to a long period of hospital care and rehabilitation during which time, for reasons that are unapparent, he was neither contacted by yourself nor your Human Resources department to advise him of him employment status. In fact, it was only when our client attempted to return to his office that he found his access rights were denied and latterly that his position had been filled some four months prior.

5. As far as Mrs Finds' insurance claim, this was denied on the grounds that Mr Finds was not dead. As far as Mr Finds' employment this has been denied him because he died in service. I'm sure you can see the contradiction here.

Doug, it is not for me to advise you in these

matters, you have your own legal team to do this and I'm sure you have spent many hours calculating that the potential loss and risk in adopting this position makes it worthwhile for your company to do so. But for a company, such as yours, that markets itself as a family concern, one that promotes family values yet fails to show any compassion to one of its most senior employees who has been through what can only be the most traumatic experience one can imagine, it surely would not reflect well should this get to court.

Mr Finds himself is becoming somewhat of a media figure and, while I caution him not to go public until we sort out the details of our settlement, I fear that prolonging this issue will make that more difficult. He is daily turning down requests for television appearances, public appearances, there is even talk of him throwing out the first pitch should the Phillies get to the ACLS and while this sideshow, if I can call it that, is an inconvenient detail it is one that daily becomes an ever growing canker that needs to be excised.

So Doug, can I suggest you reconvene with your team and come back to us with a fair and equitable settlement that covers the issues of termination, death in service and the life insurance within the next seven days.

Yours sincerely

Thomas H. L. Pinkerton

Laz held the letter in his hand, his mouth open, his hand shaking.

"Great letter, huh?" said Scott Breslin, clearly proud of the document he had crafted.

"Wow," said Laz. "They want me to throw out the pitch at the ALCS?"

"What? No, don't be stupid," said the lawyer. "I made that up. Jeez..."

"But you say here," Laz protested "'there is even talk of him throwing out the first pitch should the Phillies get to the ACLS...'"

"OK, fine!" said Scott. "I'm talking about it 'Hey Laz, wanna throw out the first pitch at the ALCS. Laz, if we get there, how's about you throw the first pitch?' Happy now?"

"Shit..." said Laz, suddenly not excited any more. "I was really looking forward to that."

"My God..." sighed Scott. "How about the rest of the letter?"

"Yeah" sighed Laz running over it one more time. "It seems fine... Do you think it'll work?"

"Honestly," sighed the lawyer, "best case scenario, they'll treat it like a redundancy. Work out a package based on your salary and years of service, maybe invite you in and 'retire' you officially, give you a clock or some such."

"Fuck them," said Laz. "I wouldn't go near the place after what they've put me through?"

"Trust me," advised Scott, "you'll go. You'll smile, take the clock, make nice, then run like hell to cash the check and put the clock on E-bay. You'll go."

"When are you sending it?" Laz was already counting off when the seventh day would be.

"Tonight," said the lawyer. "I just have to get Pinkerton to sign it."

"How come you're not signing it?"

"How come? If they saw my name on it, they wouldn't even look at it." Scott laughed. "They see Thomas H. L. Pinkerton on it, they'll sit up and read it at least."

"Will he sign it?" Laz asked, cognizant that he had always read everything he signed at Yours Mutual.

"Of course"

"Will he read it?"

"No!" laughed the lawyer, "do you think he checks any of

the work I do for him?"

Breslin looked at Laz like he was an innocent

"Tell me, when you would come and see T.P. and pay your
$2,500 an hour, did you think he ever did any of the work
you paid him for? No way, he just farms it out to us little
mice. You just saved yourself $2,250, Laz!"

THE LINE

IT WAS FOUR days and many phone calls to Scott Breslin later and Laz was driving around downtown Philly when his phone rang. He picked up, after a glancing quickly from one side to another to make sure no cops were about.

"Laz, it's me, Scott. I just had a minute between meetings and I thought I would give you a quick call..."

"Did they get back to us?" Laz responded excitedly, still paranoiacally looking from side-to-side.

"No, I'm just calling to say they have not gotten back to us and to remind you what I've already told you a hundred times, that I will call you as soon as I hear anything OK?" replied Scott testily.

"Yeah, OK," replied Laz wearily.

"And another thing," added the lawyer before hanging up, "you are still not throwing out the opening pitch at the ALCS."

"Funny." said Laz, but the lawyer was already gone.

Laz eased the Audi through the late morning rush hour. Philly traffic was never that bad, unless you took in the Schuylkill Expressway, or 'Sure-Kill' as it was known, but downtown these uncoordinated traffic signals and stop signs were a killer, especially in this part of town. Plus, every stop sign or traffic light seemed to have a potential mugger or shooter hanging off it and Laz repeatedly flicked the auto-lock on his center console. His phone rang again. He grabbed at it.

"Did they call?"

"Did who call, Lazarus?" asked Mary.

"Oh it's you..." he answered deflatedly.

"You don't sound too excited about it..." replied Mary.

He thought about this for a second and wondered what planet his wife was living on right now, what concept of reality she currently had a grasp of. "I should be pleased why?" he sighed.

"You should be pleased Lazarus, because..." Mary sounded genuinely excited, "we've rushed through the paperwork!"

Laz shook his head as he looked for and then made his next turn.

"What paperwork?" he asked.

It was Mary's turn to sigh. "Why our settlement silly! It's ready for you to sign. You just need to go by the lawyers and put your John Hancock on it!"

Divorces and break-ups are supposed to be sad and emotional events, thought Lazarus. There is supposed to be a lot of wailing and gnashing of teeth, or was that going to hell? Oh well, they were pretty much the same thing he thought. But Mary seemed practically gleeful. He'd never seen or heard her this happy. If the only way he could make her happy, he thought, was by leaving her maybe he was doing the right thing.

"Put my 'what' on it?" he hated that expression, but his wife always used it.

"Your *John Hancock* Laz! Your signature," she explained.

Laz sighed, no good would come out of fighting this, though he was conscious he hadn't even consulted his lawyer. All he had was a gash on his head and a possible concussion, he was probably malnourished and definitely depressed. But he was tired, tired of it all. He was playing his last hand and he didn't know what to do if he lost this one.

"Alright, Mary," he told her. "I'll go by Pinkerton's and sign the damn thing."

He heard an intake of breath as he pulled the car to the curb.

"Oh Laz, I didn't use Pinkerton," Mary clarified. "I thought that might be awkward. Awkward, and embarrassing, for you dear."

"So where do I go then?" he said exasperated.

"Frost, Rodgers and Pennington on Locust Street." Mary

waited for his reaction.

"Frost, Rodgers and Pennington..." Laz repeated. It seemed quite familiar but he couldn't quite think why. He repeated it again, almost inaudibly, "Frost, Rodgers and Pennington..."

"That's right dear..." Mary's voice wavered a little.

Laz spoke slowly, "Isn't that Aubrey's law firm?" he asked.

"Aubrey who dear?" she hadn't called him 'dear' for years but now she was using it all the time.

"Aubrey Fink, from my club," he reminded her.

"IS IT?" She tried to sound impressed. "Oh, then they must be good then, mustn't they?"

Laz was annoyed. He was a fool but he didn't like being treated like one. "Oh come on Mary, don't come the innocent with me, I know you've been fucking him for years! So give me credit for some intelligence..."

"Lazarus Finds, how dare you?" she screamed.

"Mary, everyone's told me, so get over yourself," Laz shouted back. "Just try being honest with me for once."

There was a long pause when both parties felt the other might have already hung up but neither wanted to say are you still there? Eventually it was Mary who spoke.

"I'm sorry Laz, Aubrey felt it was better to use his lawyers. Once you sign this, no further claims. It's all done. Be there by Tuesday or they all have to be done again. Tuesday, Laz."

"What about the children?" he asked. "Do I need to come by and see them?"

"Probably best not to, not just yet. And don't go to Devon this weekend, Aubrey's taking Judith."

"I hate the Devon fucking horse show," said Lazarus hanging up the phone.

He rested his head on the steering wheel for what seemed a long time. This was all for the best he told himself, all for the best. He had a new life just around the corner, a better life. He got out of the car, double and triple locked it and looked up at the building. St Jude's House.

The queue for the mission stretched around the corner. Laz slowly walked up and down scanning for Tiffany but couldn't see her. The doors opened at noon which was still an hour away. Already there must have been a hundred, maybe a hundred and fifty people in line. He was worried. What if something had happened to her? But then, maybe she stayed overnight? She probably had. Maybe he should get her a cell phone, or would that be dangerous? Would she get mugged for that? He didn't want to place her in any more danger than she already was in. He might ask that guy on reception, Joshua, he was an animal but at least he seemed to care about her.

The wide array of humankind awaiting the impending opening amazed him. From young kids, teenagers, who clearly hadn't washed in weeks and wearing rags that barely clung to their bodies, to middle aged women who wouldn't look out of place pushing a trolley out of Wegmans, men in not so shabby suits who might have been on their way to work and a lot of angry people who seemed to feel the world had betrayed them. Laz had a lot more in common with these people than he had thought.

He was suddenly was conscious of hundreds of eyes upon him. It wasn't that he wasn't the only non-black guy there, there were quite a few whites and latinos in the line, a few orientals and asians too, but he was the only one walking up and down looking at faces and he probably looked remarkably 'copish' . A couple of times, to try and normalize the situation, he tried saying something like "I'm looking for my daughter," to which the reply was invariably along the lines of "She don't want to see you daddy," or "Try under the Ben Franklin," a notorious red-light area.

Eventually Laz gave up and decided to return to the car and check back after the shelter had opened its doors.

THE CHECK

JOSHUA WAS STILL at his post in reception, now reading in the Daily News how the Phillies still had a shot at the wild card spot. Laz stood in front of him and waited as the receptionist ignored him.

"So, do you think they still have a shot?" He threw it out there like a pitch. It landed about three feet short. Joshua looked up.

"What the fuck are you doing back here?"

"Um," Laz answered nervously, "I need to see Tiffany. Please."

"Are you kidding me joker?" Joshua leaned back in his chair. "After what happened last time? There's no way she'd want to see you!"

"And I would understand that," agreed Laz, "and that would be fine with me. I would just want to give her the opportunity of knowing I was here"

"And if she said no?" asked the big man.

"I'd go," said Laz, "promise."

"Piss off!" the receptionist told him and went back to reading the sports.

Laz unfurled a twenty from his wallet and slipped it across the counter-top. "Can I make a donation?" he asked. "To the Joshua fund?"

The man slowly looked up, around and then over his shoulder. He smiled a big white and somewhat toothless smile. "Well, why didn't you say so?" he beamed. "Wait here. I'll see what I can do," and with that he disappeared down the dark corridor towards the back of the building.

Laz waited and while he did he looked around him. The walls were covered with various mementos, pictures and photos, of past residents perhaps, Laz thought. One of the walls was filled with a homemade paper barometer from a failed fund raising drive, with the red mercury line only filled three-quarters the way up. There were letters pinned onto a grubby cork noticeboard written by grateful souls and scrawled on anything that would take paper or ink. One in particular caught his eye. It read "I wanna tank Mis Tifney fur al she dun fur me." Laz wondered if it was his Tiffany. He was sure it was.

He had only waited five minutes or so but the lost souls of humanity drifted past him, laughing, talking to each other, talking to themselves, glaring at him remembering him from before perhaps, some praying, some just looking plain scared. We're not so different Laz thought, we have the same problems, they just come in different wrapping paper. Presently Joshua arrived back and beckoned him to follow.

"OK, I found her and she agreed to see you," the big guy advised. " But if you upset her..."

"I know, I know," continued Laz. "You'll kick my ass all the way from here to 69th Street!"

"Exactly," confirmed Joshua. "Just so we understand each other. And we'll keep the 'donation' just to ourselves?"

"Of course," agreed Lazarus.

Joshua led him down through the dark and dank corridors, it all seemed vaguely familiar to him now and eventually showed him to the same office he'd been in the time before.

"Here he is Miss Tiffany. You just holler if he causes any ruckus!"

"I will Joshua," Tiffany promised. "Don't you you worry about me. I can handle this one."

Laz entered the office, scene of his histrionics on his last visit, Tiffany – his daughter – had seated herself behind the desk this time. Probably for safety, he thought.

"Sorry about last time," he said awkwardly.

She nodded. "Did you want to sit down?" she asked coolly.

He sat down opposite her. Each waited for the other one to say something. It was the girl who broke the silence.

"Joshua said you wanted to see me about something?"

Lazarus cleared his throat. "Yes, it was nice of him to give us the office again."

Tiffany looked confused, "how do you mean?"

"For the privacy?" Laz suggested.

"Privacy?" Tiffany now seemed more confused.

Lazarus could see that the girl had not picked up on the subtleties and nuance in Joshua's gesture, in allowing them to have to office so as not to be disturbed.

"Yes, him allowing us to use the office, to be alone." Laz tried to say it as clearly as possible.

Tiffany looked Laz straight in the eye. "This is my office."

"Your office?" answered Laz totally bemused.

"My office," confirmed Tiffany.

"They give you an office?" Laz's mind spun wildly unable to figure out why the girl would get an office.

"They give me an office," her turn to be patient and speak slowly. "Are you going to repeat everything I say"

Laz spat it out. "But why?" and then over her shoulder he saw several framed certificates with her name on it; one a Bachelor of Arts from Drexel, another a Masters from Penn and a Social Work PhD from Widener where he himself had gone to business school.

"Because I am the Director of the St Jude House." Laz's mouth hung open, again. "Why what did you think?" she asked.

"I thought," stammered Laz, "I thought..." he struggled to breathe. "I thought you lived here..."

"Well" sighed Tiffany "I practically do!"

Lazarus slowly regained his composure. How come he hadn't seen any of this on his last visit, it was all in plain sight, but he was so wrapped up in himself and locked in his preconceptions of her, of the other people here, he never thought... But that was always his problem, wasn't it? He told himself, he never could think, he never could see what was staring him in the face.

"I'm sorry Tiffany. I'm a fool" he apologized.

She shook her head and smiled at him. "Not at all, I take it as a compliment."

"So what brings you here today Laz?" she asked.

Laz reached inside his pocket and pulled out a white letter-sized envelope, which he started tapping on the desk.

"Well," he laughed. "It all seems terribly embarrassing now. You see, I thought you were, well, one of them," gesturing outside the office, "and I was trying to think what I could do to help you. So I took out a thousand dollars and I was going to give it to you so you could get some new clothes or stuff for your place, the place where you live."

Tiffany reached across the desk and took the envelope, slid open a side drawer and dropped it in.

"I'll take it! Thanks."

Laz could barely speak. "But, but you don't need it!"

"Laz trust me," she told him. "I need it more that you know and if I were 'one of them' as you put it, I would spend that money in all the wrong places and it would be gone in two nights, and it sure as hell wouldn't be spent on clothes or *my apartment,* and I would be a whole lot worse off for it."

"But, if you don't need it," he protested.

"Yes, I do need it!" she insisted. "I can feed two hundred people for three days on that if I'm careful. Can you imagine that? Think of the good that money's gonna do."

Laz nodded unconvinced, still thinking he probably needed it more. "Can I get a tax receipt?" he asked.

"Of course," she answered, "next February. Now what the hell happened to your head?"

Laz told her the whole story and Tiffany listened sympathetically.

"So after she kicked me out and hit me over the head, my one best friend told me she'd been sleeping with my other best friend for the last two years! So much for best friends huh?" he concluded.

"Man, I caused a whole lot of mess going to your funeral didn't I?" confessed Tiffany.

Laz waved that thought away, "No, no. Don't ever think that. If you'd never come, I'd never have found you and right now you're the best thing in my life."

"Then you are having one shitty life, Mister!" Tiffany concluded. They both laughed. "I told my Momma I saw you," she confessed.

Laz's eye's opened wide. "You did! What did she say?"

"She beat the living daylights outta me," the girl said all serious and went to lift up her top. "Do you wanna see the bruises?"

"Really?" cried Laz.

Tiffany slumped back into her chair. "Of course she didn't, stupid! She's a biology professor. She don't go beating up her children!"

"Biology professor?" Laz brightened. "Which university?"

"No Laz!" admonished Tiffany. "Drop it. She's happy. She says doesn't want to know you. Now come on, let me show you around."

The St Jude's House kitchen wasn't up to much, it was really not much more than an ante-room to the dining hall, even the dining hall wasn't so much a dining hall as a long rectangular space with rows of trestle tables and benches set alongside them. The kitchen equipment was pretty basic, nothing like you'd expect to find in a restaurant or even a school, no deep fryers here, no grills, no walk in freezers or refrigerators. Tiffany explained how the whole process worked.

"We do a lot of canned food, potatoes, tomatoes, peas, other vegetables. I know it's not good, way too much salt in it, but we can't afford fresh. Sometimes we get the stuff the supermarkets are throwing away but it's not great, the potatoes can be pretty spongy, even moldy, the bread is good for a day or two. We have a connection to the local church and parishioners will make and freeze food for us in large aluminum trays that we supply them with."

Laz gestured to a mountain of silver foil in the corner, "like those?"

"Just like those. In fact..." she half whispered. "Those are going back out again. Strictly speaking we shouldn't re-use them, but we have to. We just can't afford new ones all the time"

Laz noticed the silver trays coming out of the fridge and into the ovens. "And is the food good?" he asked.

Tiffany laughed. "It really varies, but you play to people's strengths, We had this lady, Mrs Rossi, I swear she used to put a whole tub of garlic salt into her lasagna and she would send the same thing week after week and we had to throw it away, even Joshua wouldn't eat it and he'll eat anything. Then," she continued conspiratorially "one Sunday she sends canolis and they were amazing! So we got word back through the priest how she made everybody's week with the canolis. Now we always get canolis! Thank God!"

Laz watched the kitchen staff buzzing backwards and forwards, "The team works well, have they been together long?"

"About ten minutes" advised Tiffany. "They're volunteers. Some are housewives who've driven down here before school pick up, others are office workers like you who once or twice a week choose to do this in their lunch hour, some have been on the street and are back on their feet but come back here to give something back."

"Wow!" said Laz thinking that all he'd ever done in his lunch hour was have a cocktail or two, he'd never dreamed of doing something like this or that people even did this. "So how does it work then, you do lunch…"

"Well," Tiffany explained, "we have a few full time staff but we're completely dependent on our volunteers. We feed about three hundred souls a day, up to 750 meals. We start with breakfast at seven for sleep overs…"

"You do sleep overs?" Laz questioned.

"Sure, we have 60 beds. I wish we had more, but we're packed. If you register at noon and stay for the afternoon programs you can have a bed for the night."

"So you could live here then?" he suggested.

Tiffany shook her head. "No, unfortunately we're not that sort of facility. But you can stay up to three nights while you sort yourself out."

"And after breakfast?" asked Laz. Lunch was in full flow now, it seemed like a stew or something, with bread . It was being gobbled up.

"Chores... time to pay the piper," Tiffany continued. "Changing sheets, sweeping floors, cleaning the bathrooms.

"I bet that goes down well!" snorted Laz.

"It does. It's work. Most of these people just want meaning, just want worth. Any type of work makes them feel valued." She looked Laz in the face. "Do you know I've seen a man cry just because I said he did a great job cleaning a toilet?"

Laz could only shake his head, but he understood. When was the last time someone had said he had done something well?

"Doors open at twelve, lunch at one. We have counsellors available all afternoon."

"Counsellors?"

"Sure, if they have a problem, medical, legal, personal, there's someone here to help them. Most of them can't help themselves and get in more trouble if they try."

"I suppose they could…" nodded Laz.

"And then dinner at six," she concluded.

"Are they allowed to have been drinking?" asked Laz.

"Absolutely not" Tiffany immediately answered. "They'd be out of control. They'd be no discipline and soon they'd all be at it. Strict rules! No drinking, no drugs!"

"But what if they're hungry?" Laz asked, totally sympathetic to the hungry drunk.

"Well, we're not heartless," Tiffany confided. "We'll slip them a sandwich if we can, but they know they're missing out by not being here."

They wandered on. "I saw you pretty drunk more than once," she confessed. "I used to follow you to that club of yours and watch you through the window. Pretty sad."

Laz shook his head. "Proper little stalker weren't you?"

"For a while, yes." She looked at him, "then I decided I didn't like what I saw."

"I don't do that now," he told her quietly. "Not since the accident."

"That's good," Tiffany answered. "I'd hate to have you thrown out of here." They walked on. "And then we close at nine. That's the tough part…"

"How so?" asked Laz.

Tiffany sighed. "Not so bad in the summer, in this weather, but when it's heavy rain or freezing cold in the winter, or when someone is screaming that they don't want to go out there again because someone or something is waiting for them..." her voice trailed off. "And then sometimes they just don't come back and you wonder..." She sniffed.

"And then," she continued brightly, "they'll be a blizzard and you say 'screw it' and tell them, 'OK everyone, back inside and don't tell anyone you stayed here tonight! And behave!'"

"Is that so bad?" asked Laz.

Tiffany looked at him as if she'd trusted him with her darkest secret. "They'd shut us down if they knew Laz..."

"Oh" he said. "That would not be good."

Tiffany surveyed the progress of the lunch service. "Come on, let's grab some lunch. I'll show you off!"

They took a tray, some chili and bread, to a table where an older and youngish black man sat with an elderly white woman.

"Do you mind if we join you all? asked Tiffany.

"No dearie," said the woman. "You go right ahead," as the two men half stood and indicated Tiffany should sit between them. Laz sat across from her, next the the lady.

"This here is Mr Finds," Tiffany introduced him. "And this fine gentlemen on my right is Moses."

Laz reached across and shook his hand. "Pleased to meet you."

"May the Lord be with you, my Son!" said Moses.

"Moses is a retired preacher," Tiffany explained.

"Preacher's never retire," Moses corrected her.

"And this young gentleman on my left is..."

The man stood and leaned across. He was strong and powerful. He obviously worked out and took care of himself, must be a volunteer, thought Laz,

"...Scratch" he advised. "I'm an ex-dealer, but reformed."

The only dealers Laz knew worked on the market, so Laz had to ask . "Equities, bonds, commodities?"

Scratch furrowed his brow. "Crack, man! Where you from? I can still get you some, but I don't deal. I just take a little commission..."

Tiffany spoke to him sternly. "Commission is still dealing Scratch, how many times do I have to tell you?"

"Not if I just refer people it ain't, Miss Tiffany." Scratch corrected her.

"Moving on, this lovely lady is Martha."

Martha smiled and shook Laz by the hand.

"Martha used to be with the Post Office." Tiffany concluded the introductions.

"Until I went postal, tried to strangle my supervisor, grabbed a Walmart cart, put all my stuff in it and headed downtown," advised Martha providing some of the detail Tiffany had omitted. "That were twenty year ago now."

"Really" said Laz "how interesting!"

He tried the chili, not half bad really. "How did you get the name Scratch?" he asked.

"You really don't want to know" the other three said in unison.

"Especially when you're eating" added Martha.

"Mr Finds just made a substantial donation to St Jude's," announced Tiffany, changing the subject.

"Well…" blustered Laz.

"How much?" asked Scratch.

"Enough to feed us all dinner for the week!" informed Tiffany.

And then suddenly everyone was slapping him on the back and saying 'thank you' and 'well done' and Moses kept blessing him and Scratch was calling people over from other tables and telling them and, just like that, Laz felt pretty good about himself for the first time in a long time.

Tiffany just smiled from across the table, seeing the reaction the praise and attention had on this unhappy man that she had found, just another lost soul like so many at St Jude's, only this lost soul belonged to her.

THE PAPERS

LAZ KEPT FINDING excuses not to visit Mary's lawyer until Tuesday finally rolled around. He spent the weekend inside his room at the Radnor Motel, leaving only when Ascencion came to tidy it up, and even then he'd only slip to the Wawa for more Diet Coke, Herr's chips and dip. Dick had tried to call several times but he hadn't picked up and Laz thought Dick had come pounding on the the door once, but he wasn't sure, as he never could see through those spy holes properly.

He'd laid on the bed thinking about Judith riding at Devon. He actually used to enjoy going to the big horse show twice every year, until that season that Judith got trounced by that Rockstar's kid and then got majorly upset because she couldn't have a horse like 'her horse'.

"Judith" he tried to explain to her, "her Daddy is a major recording artist who has sold millions and millions of albums and he will always be able to buy her a better horse that I can buy you."

It hadn't worked and then Mary had started on him. He was more blunt with her. "Christ, Mary she's the daughter of a fucking rock superstar for God's sake! He could buy her fucking Secretariat if he wanted to!"

Judith had heard him and shouted back across the stand. "Secretariat can't jump, he's a thoroughbred, stupid!"

"Besides, he's dead Laz," Mary countered.

Unknowingly, the rockstar had overheard the whole thing and found it rather embarrassing and so Laz was politely asked to leave the member's stand by a steward. He'd got his revenge though by going home and torching all the rockstar's albums that he'd ever owned. Even though it was only one CD, it felt good.

 After that he was never welcome. Not asked, not welcome, not told how the girl had done at the shows. Just sign the checks, pay for the stabling and the gear and stay out of her life. He wished he's never bought her that first pony. He thought he's be opening a whole new world to her. He should have bought her a go-cart, she could have been the next Danica Patrick. Besides, race cars didn't shit all over you either. Still, the thought of Aubrey being there instead of him really gnawed at him.

And so the weekend continued. You can only watch so much golf and summer re-runs. He had no friends anymore, he wasn't about to go hang out in a bar, at least not yet, though he could see that day coming. He stared at the wallpaper, he tried to count the rows of brick up the artificial fireplace, he stared at the carpet and tried to even up the misaligned sections through the power of his mind. The sun would come up and then hours later he would watch the sunset form.

He could drive up to Valley Forge he thought, it was just a couple of miles away, and go for a long healthy walk, but he'd have to get in the car to get there and he didn't really

feel up to it. So Saturday passed into Sunday and Sunday
into Monday.

He could go down to St Jude's he thought, but what for?
Tiffany had his number, she knew his predicament. She
knew he was on his own, she could come to him if she
wanted to. Monday afternoon he started thinking about the
divorce papers, maybe he should have a lawyer look at
them?

"Mr Breslin is tied up today Mr Finds, I'm afraid," the
voice at the other end said.

"No, no," assured Laz. "It's not about the letter to Yours
Mutual or the opening pitch. It's about my wife. She's
trying to get me to sign some papers and I need some
advice..."

"He's not here Mr Finds. I've advised you of that," said the
voice.

"He is, he is there!" Laz insisted. "He's avoiding me, isn't
he?"

"Mr Hinds," said the voice, patient now, "Mr Breslin is in
court all day. I'll tell him you need to speak to him urgently
about your wife's papers and he'll call you first thing in the
morning. Is that OK?"

"OK," said Laz calming down a bit. "OK, thank you.
Make sure you do. Tomorrow morning. It's very
important!"

"Good afternoon, Mr Finds."

"Yes, good afternoon. Thank you." Laz put down the receiver feeling he'd done something a little positive. That was good, that was good, he said to himself.

The next day Scott Breslin met him in the parking lot of Frost, Rodgers and Pennington.

"Jesus H. Christ Laz," he cried, "why didn't you tell me about these papers?

"I don't know," admitted Laz, "there didn't seem much point. Everything else could be so much more important."

"Are you kidding me?" the lawyer punched him on the shoulder, "we're talking about everything you have in the world right now. Now, let me see them." He thrust out his hand.

"I haven't seen them yet," Laz admitted.

"Holy God!" the lawyer was exasperated, "you mean to tell me we're here to get something signed that we've never even seen? We need to delay."

"No!" said Laz firmly. "I want to get it done. If we have to negotiate a little, so be it, but I just want to get it done."

Breslin looked at the man imagining all he had been though and how it now seemed he just couldn't take any more. "OK, lets do this!" the lawyer agreed.

Ten minutes later they were in the board room of Frost, Rodgers and Pennington, with two copies of the agreement in front of them.

Breslin looked up. "Rodgers, can you give my client and me ten minutes to look these over please?"

Rodgers looked at his watch "Well, I can but we close at three..."

"What kind of a law firm closes at three?" asked Breslin.

"We do Sir, and have done since 1863," replied Rodgers.

"Well it's two thirty, give us ten and when you come back, can you get Mrs Finds on the phone. We may need her." answered Breslin.

"We will?" asked Laz.

"We may," said Breslin.

Rodgers left and Breslin under his breath said "Three o'clock, boy oh boy, did I pick the wrong firm?"

"Scott..." Laz began.

"Quiet Laz." Breslin hushed his client, "let me read through this." Lazarus sat patiently while the lawyer scanned page after page, looked up, looked around, then began again at the beginning.

"You know something Laz?" he said.

"What's that?" Laz answered, finally relieved to be allowed to speak.

"This is not half a bad deal..."

"Really?" said Laz "you think so?

"But why?" said the lawyer.

Laz sighed. "Because they think I'm finished?" he suggested.

"You know what, Laz? I think you're right – and that's great!" The lawyer rubbed his hands like a praying mantis or a, well, lawyer would do.

"Thanks a lot" said Laz.

"So here's how it breaks down: Family home, probably worth one point two, she'd get that anyway, three quarters of your portfolio, as of yesterday that was worth about eight hundred so she get's six, half of what's in the bank, that's about eighty, so she get's forty. She gets the Merc, you get the Audi. Not a bad dead."

"Sorry?" said Laz. "I know I do sound a bit crazy, but how is that a good deal for me? She gets the house, $600k in stock and $40k cash and I get $200k stock and $40 cash?"

"Yes," said the lawyer excitedly, "but you never have to pay her another penny. "If you were paying maintenance, you'd be paying $150,000 a year to her until the children are through college – Aubrey's going to be paying that now."

Laz's eye widened, "Ah, I see..."

"But we have to get this done quickly Laz, because this is based on your situation today," Breslin advised.

"So?" Laz failed to see the distinction.

The lawyer hurried on, "Say, just suppose we manage to do some deal with Yours Mutual, it's quite reasonable to assume that that is not part of this deal and whatever deal we strike with YM is, quite fairly and legally, all yours. Understand?"

"I understand." Laz liked this kid.

Just then Mr Rodgers walked back in. "Is everything in order Gentlemen?"

"Pretty much," said Breslin. "Just one thing, Mr Finds wants the Mercedes, Mrs Finds can have the Audi."

"No I don't" hissed Laz. "I love the Audi!"

Breslin leaned into him. "The Merc is payed off Laz, you still own $45k on the Audi..."

"I want the Merc!" shouted Laz at Rodgers and Mary.

Rodgers spoke into his mobile phone.

"Mrs Finds says that's not a problem," the wife's lawyer confirmed. "She asks that she can she keep the car until after the Concours d'Elegance at Ridley? She's entered it apparently?"

Breslin looked stumped. "It's a posh car show at the Hunt in August," Laz explained, "and gentleman's car rally"

"Is that a problem?" asked Mr Rodgers.

"Not at all," advised Laz.

"Then let's amend and sign!" said Breslin.

THE COP

SCOTT BRESLIN, FEELING very pleased with himself, left Laz in the parking lot of Frost, Rodgers and Pennington. Laz didn't know how he felt. He was grateful to Scott for helping him through a situation that he would have made a complete hash of himself and he realized, through the lawyer's nimble footwork, he had made himself an extra 45k at the end there, but he loved his Audi and would miss it.

Images of the last six months or so raced through his mind. He imagined, though he couldn't remember falling down the grand curved staircase at his lovely home, a home he would probably never enter again. He remember Dick being the first to tell him of so-called fatal fall at home, and then being found barely alive in a coffin on its way to the crematorium fire. He recalled the embarrassment of being rejected and ejected from his own club, his refuge for these last twenty or so years and then the humiliation of his excision, that's all he could call it, from the firm he had devoted his life to. He tempered that with finding he had a new daughter, but that hadn't improved things that much and her mother had vowed to have nothing to do with him. Then, discovering that one of his two best friends was having an affair with his own wife, while the other was covering it up and last, but not least, his wife of twenty two years had taken practically everything he had and left him with almost nothing! How could it get any worse? The tears of self-pity began to flow.

At some point there was a tap an the window, Laz ignored it, he didn't want Breslin to see him like this, then another one, much more insistent this time and almost pounding. Then a loud and commanding voice. "Hey Buddy! Open this window!" Laz looked up. It was a Police Officer. "Open this window" he said again "and do it now!"

Laz reached for the control, admiring the solid wood grain arm rests of the Audi while he still could as he wound down the window.

"I'm sorry Officer, what seems to be the trouble?" he asked trying to gather his composure. He noticed for the first time a police cruiser pulled up beside him and wondered how long it had been there.

"Don't you know you can't park here?" replied the policeman. Laz was indignant, Main Line police had a reputation for being over protective of their townships and overstepping the mark with outsiders, but Laz was still one of them.

"If you don't mind Officer," Laz responded haughtily. "I just came out of a meeting with Mr Rodgers of Frost, Rodgers and Pennington." That'll show him, thought Laz. It was just then Laz realized that the officer was shining a flashlight in his face and that it had gotten remarkably dark for a mid-summer's afternoon. An eclipse perhaps?

"This business closed at three o'clock buddy, it's after ten now." the officer informed Laz. "Step out of the vehicle."

Laz climbed out of the car totally bemused, could it really be that late? Had he blacked out, or had he just been sitting there?

"Have you been drinking buddy?" The policeman leaned close and cautiously sniffed Laz's breath.

""I don't drink," Laz replied, pleased for once that after the many times previously he'd been stopped and tried to use that line, he could now mean it. The policeman shone the flashlight into Laz's face again. Laz shied away.

"Have you been, um, crying?" asked the cop.

Laz didn't really know how to answer that. He seemed to remember that he had, but that could have been hours ago, but then again it could just have been five minutes.

"Possibly?" was the best he could offer.

"Sir," the officer suggested "you seem rather upset. Did someone die"

Laz thought about saying I did, but figured there was a one hundred percent chance that would get him arrested and thrown in jail, though that might be preferable to returning to the Radnor Motel.

"Sir, is there someone I can call? Someone who could come and get you?"

Laz considered whether it was a positive going from being a *Buddy* to a *Sir.* He thought about all the cop movies he'd seen and thought *Sir* one step towards the friendly side. Laz shook his head from side to side,

"Not any more officer," he told the cop. "They've all left me. I'm all alone."

The policeman looked up and down the street, then back to Laz.

"I tell you what," the cop put his hand on Laz's shoulder, "it's about my break time. How about you and I go over to Mo's Diner there, get a free coffee and doughnut and you can tell me all about it?"

Laz raised his head, just enough to look the officer in the eye and weakly replied, "OK."

Fifteen minutes later Laz was feeling a lot better. This Officer Mike Murphy was a great guy and these free coffees and doughnuts were awesome. He was just finishing his tale of woe as they topped off his cup for the second time.

"That is quite a story." said Murphy. "Make sure you sign my napkin before you leave. Hey, you know I remember seeing it now on CNN!"

"I will, I'll be sure to," said Laz, pleased to be cashing in on his fame and half hoping Mike would introduce him to the rest of the crowd. But he didn't.

"But let me tell you," Officer Murphy continued, "you don't realize it now but that wife of your's is doing you the biggest fucking favor you can imagine."

"How do you figure that?" asked Laz.

"OK, my case," explained Mike, "on the force twenty years, married fifteen, coming up to retirement in ten. She knew I was a cop when we married right? Right?"

"Er, right," answered Laz not realizing it was incumbent on him to verify the facts of the story as the cop went along.

"But every day she's bitching at me for being at work too long, not spending more time with her, not going out, not staying in, not walking the fucking dog. So what do I do? What do I do?" asked the cop.

"Er, I do not know?" replied Laz

"I'll tell you what I do. Hey Mo! Another doughnut here for my friend," said Mike. "I'll tell you what I do. One day I get off work early, pick up some flowers and a bottle of wine, I let myself in the house and what is she doing?"

Laz didn't wait to be prompted, "walking the dog?" he suggested.

"Fucking the guy from the deli!" cried Officer Mike.

"Oh!" Laz shrank back a little bit.

"So what did I do?"

"Well I'm sure you didn't give her the flowers." Laz

speculated.

"Damn straight I didn't," replied the cop. "I pulled my gun out, just to scare him mind, then chased him round the house 'til I caught him. She was screaming like a fucking banshee, and I got hold of him and I said to him the only way you get out of here alive Tony, is if you take that bitch with you, and he did"

"And you had no clue?" asked Laz.

The cop thought. "Only that she seemed to smell of pastrami all the time."

"And you've been happy ever since?" Laz asked him.

"Sure have," confirmed the cop. "Got a girlfriend twenty years younger than me who screws me like a crazy woman. I don't have a fucking dog to walk anymore. Only thing is I can't go to my favorite deli anymore and I have to go to goddamn Mario's now which is another half a mile down the street and their salami sucks."

"I'm not sure I could handle a girlfriend twenty years younger," confessed Laz.

Officer Mike Murphy slapped him on the back. "You don't understand Laz, you don't have to do that. Your whole world starts to open up again. You can do anything you want!"

Laz thought about that for a minute and then said, "I suppose I can."

"Of course you can!" said the cop and then pushing Laz's coffee cup back towards the counter told him. "Now go and move your damn car!"

"OK" said Laz nodding. "I know what I'm going to do."

THE AMBUSH

LAZ WAS SEATED in the Audi parked outside St Jude's waiting for Tiffany to get off. He realized all manner of things could go wrong that would detain her, but generally he knew that she left at nine when they closed the doors for the night. This night, being a particularly fine summer's evening, most of the attendees of that evening's supper had already hightailed it someplace else, so hopefully...

It didn't take long and at five after the hour Tiffany appeared and headed towards the 69th Street Transit Center. He hopped out of the car, as nimbly as his still recovering body would allow.

"Tiffany" he cried after her "it's me, Laz!" he hurried to catch up. "Can I have a quick word?"

In his hand he held another white envelope. She stood with her hands on her hips. Was this her attack position, he wondered?

"Are you stalking me now Laz?" she asked him.

"No, no," he puffed. He could feel the ache in his leg where he had broken it and his head throbbed where he'd been hit. "No. I needed to give you something and I didn't want to bother you at work."

"Them your wheels Mr F?" said a voice in the shadows on

the corner.

Laz peered into the murkiness, but could just see a vague outline of someone.

"It's Scratch" advised Tiffany.

"Oh," said Laz, then turning to the darkness replied. "Yes, the silver Audi RS6... it's mine."

"Shame," replied the darkness. "I was gonna have me them twenties..."

"Twenties?" Laz asked Tiffany.

"Your wheels, your 20 inch alloy wheels," Tiffany instructed. "He was going to steal them..."

"How do you know this?" Laz whispered.

Tiffany just cocked her head and gave him a where do you think I've been all my life look.

"Scratch" she said. "Can you keep and eye on the car for us? We'll just be a minute."

"Sure thing Miss Tiffany," said the voice in the darkness. "Anything for Mr F."

"You're a God around here now, you know," she told Laz.

"Really?" Laz puffed up a bit. "Wow!"

"What's with the envelope Laz," she asked. "You don't need to make another donation."

Laz looked at the envelope. It wasn't addressed, just a plain white letter-sized envelope with the Radnor Motel logo in the top left corner. He twirled it around in his fingers like a drum major with a baton.

"Listen Tiffany," he started a speech he'd practiced several times in the car on the way down here. "I know your mother doesn't want to see me..."

"Laz..." she tried to stop him.

Laz held up his hand. "Please, please, just hear me out. I know you mother doesn't want to see me. I've accepted that, just as I accepted her disappearing twenty seven years ago. I got over it then, I'll get over it now. I hope you and I can carve out some kind of relationship."

Laz's hands went backwards and forwards in a sort of sawing motion and Tiffany nodded.

He continued. "And I know how she has her own life now and I am so happy for her, SO happy for her, no one deserves it more than she does. No one."

Tiffany nodded again, but there were tears in her eyes.

"And I don't want to change that or upset her, but I just wanted to close that chapter from twenty seven years ago." Laz's eye's welled up now. "Because you see we left so many things left unsaid, so many things left undone, so many things we felt inside we never got to say."

Tiffany wiped at her eyes. "Laz, I'm so sorry to have put you through all of this. I wish I'd never have gone to your stupid funeral"

Laz grabbed her hands. "No, no, no. No, don't say that Tiffany. If you hadn't had gone I would never have found out about you, and your mother.. Plus the attendance would have been 15% lower."

She laughed.

"Tiffany?" Laz pleaded. "Please take her the letter. You can read it first if you want. It's not sealed. And you can decide whether you give it to her. But at least take the letter, even if I think you've delivered it I'll feel better."

She slowly reached out and took the letter from his fingers, she too twirled it around before putting it in her purse. "I don't know what I'll do with it," she told him before taking his hands and holding them to her chest, "but you deserve better than all this. You deserve a good life, a great life. But going back twenty five plus years to something that had barely started isn't the solution, Dad."

They stood there holding each other for a few moments, trembling, eyes wet with tears.

"You called me Dad" he said at length.

She paused for a moment then answered "I know. Well you are, aren't you?"

A voice in the darkness spoke for both of them . "Man, that is the saddest thing I ever heard" said Scratch.

"Just keep your eyes on the wheels Scratch!" said Tiffany.

THE BOARD MEETING

THE CHAIRMAN AND CEO of Yours Mutual, Doug Dangle, breezed into the boardroom on the 16th floor on the corner of Market and 15th. He swung around the assembled officers and headed for his reserved spot at the head of the table, where he had a spectacular view of the city and was eye-to-eye with William Penn atop City Hall. Dick was among those already assembled, as well as Clarence Causley from HR, Jim Z from Marketing and Trevor Berry, CFO and Dangle's general dogsbody.

Dangle didn't wait to sit down before he opened up. "Ok let's get this ridiculous meeting done with so we can get back to work and earn some real money. Posman?

"Very well" Dick started. "We're here to discuss the letter sent by Lazarus Find's lawyers, Pinkerton's times three and Smythe."

"Bullshit letter," interjected Dangle. "Fucking bullshit letter!"

"That's as maybe," continued Dick. He paused for a moment. "May I just suggest that, since I was once good friends with Laz, that I recluse myself from this conversation?"

Dangle looked at Dick Posman and started to turn puce.

"What am I supposed to do?" he asked. "Pull another lawyer out of my fucking hat?"

"Well, er…" Dick stammered.

Dangle leaned forward. "Are you still friends with the jerk?" he demanded.

Dick shook his head. "No, we don't even speak."

"No fucking problem then," assured the Chairman. "Continue."

Dick took a deep breath. "We had been requested by PPP and S to respond within seven days. It's now been nearly three weeks."

"Yeah! Fuck that!" sneered Dangle. "That little twerp thinks he can push us around?" The Chairman looked over at the CFO who was busily writing. "Don't fucking minute that Trevor, Christ! Carry on Dick."

"Anyway, it's interesting in that they are not making a specific claim."

"How so?" the Chairman was interested.

Clarence Causley interjected. "If I may. They want a settlement on Termination, Death in Service and Life Insurance, but they don't say what exactly. They're leaving the ball in our court."

"Great" said Dangle. "So let's take it to the People's fucking

Court and they can decide!"

"Is that a good idea?" asked Dick.

"Why the hell not? Dangle shook his head. "What's wrong with you people? We are a fucking Goliath and he is..." he turned to Trevor again. "Who was the little nerdy guy, Trevor?"

"David," advised Trevor.

"Yeah," Dangle exclaimed. "He's a tiny, weeny David..."

"David slew Goliath" Trevor clarified.

"He what?" said Dangle.

"The little nerdy guy won." Everyone was nodding.

Dick motioned to Jim Z, the PR guy.

"Hi Doug, Jimmy Z." He introduced himself as he always did. Jim's surname was some Polish name that nobody could ever pronounce so he was called 'Jim Z' or just plain 'Zee'. Like every PR and Marketing guy, Zee was always working his room. "Doug, as you may know, we are launching a huge $80 million campaign next month. One that is planned to reposition Yours Mutual as the world's 'caring' insurance company."

"Yeah so?" Dangle lit up a cigar. "I signed the fucking check already."

"Doug," Clarence protested. "This is a non-smoking building."

"Shut up Clarence and find me an ashtray," the CEO told him. "I can't think if I can't smoke"

"OK Doug, sure," answered Clarence as he started opening credenza doors.

"Continue!" Doug waved Zee on.

Jim flicked on the TV and started his powerpoint.

Dangle sighed. "Not a fucking Powerpoint, we won't be out of here before lunch now!"

"The basis of the campaign are five seemingly unrelated, but subtlety linked, TV ads. The first one here shows the Yours Mutual rep actually sitting shiva and giving the widow the insurance check before he leaves."

He played the tape, the widow was grieving, the agent was in a beautiful Brooks Brothers suit, he prayed, cried a little, dabbed his eyes, walked to the widow, they hugged, he slipped her an envelope, she tilted her head to one side and mouthed, "Thank you."

The executives nodded their approval, the chairman looked up to the ceiling.

Jim went on to the next slide "This next one demonstrates the importance of having an employment protection plan, in case you can't work."

Jim pushed play and, somewhat unfortunately, this commercial showed a man with an impossibly angled leg lying at the foot of the stairs holding a paintbrush in his hand while the voice over talked about the necessity of having an accident protection plan because, 'Your company may not care as much about you as we do at Yours Mutual.'"

There was a groan from the room and Dangle said, "Just tell me about the others"

Jim Z nodded. "I'm afraid the third one talks about how all types of insurance help keep your family safe and protected. Mr Finds family just split apart, mostly because we bailed on them I believe..."

"A matter of opinion," the chairman disagreed.

Jim hurriedly continued. "The fourth one speaks about how we are a big company with small town values and the final one sells us as the insurance company with a heart." Zee paused. More groans from around the room.

"In a nutshell," Dick summarized, "in the case of Laz Finds, Yours Mutual went against every one of these core values that we are trying to espouse in this media campaign"

"Eighty million big ones," Jim Z reminded them.

"Is that all?" said Dangle. "Can't we re-edit?"

Jim shook his head. "And we have a newspaper and magazine blitz booked starting next month based on these same concepts"

Doug Dangle thought for a moment. "But do people really know his story?"

Jim thought for a few moments. "It got a lot of play on the news channels, CNN and CNBC anyway. Fox News didn't cover it so much because of the Tea Party Convention."

"Well that's it!" said the CEO. "We'll pull the ads from CNN, no one watches fucking CNBC anyway, put extra media buys on FOX News, 'cause their red neck viewers only ever watch Fox News, and we'll be fine!"

Doug looked around the table and there was general nodding and agreement, the only one not nodding was Dick Posman.

"What is it Dick?" asked the chairman.

"Well," said Dick, "I had hoped we would decide this case on its merits, decide what was right and not be swayed by outside influences or their potential negative, even potentially calamitous impact on our business."

"Spit it out, Posman!" Dangle ordered.

"Well, the very last time I saw Laz," Dick advised the group, "in fact, the very last time he ever spoke to me. There was talk of..." Dick checked to ensure he had their complete attention. "There was talk of Oprah."

"Oprah!" they all sang in unison. Zee slowly put his head in his hands.

"In fact he told me he was on his way to see her that very morning," confirmed the lawyer.

"We're fucked!" said Jim Z.

"Aw shit!" said Dangle.

"Do I write this down?" asked Trevor.

"Shut up, Trevor!" ordered the Chairman. "What do we do now,?" he asked the room.

"Don't worry," said Dick. "I have a plan."

"I have some ideas too," said Jim Z.

THE OTHER LETTER

ROOM 213
THE Radnor Motel
Lancaster Avenue
Radnor, PA 19080

25th July 201_

Dear Roberta

I've sat here for over an hour now, staring at this piece of paper wondering where to start, so I'll start there. How do I begin? First of all, based on what Tiffany has said, I doubt she'll agree to give you this letter and, even if she does, I don't suppose you will ever read it.

I have so many questions, but then I can already imagine many of the answers because they are so obvious, at least now – but they weren't to me then. Back then, you just disappeared off the face of the earth and I never understood why. I looked for you, I did. I went to your dorm. Your friends didn't know where you were, they just said your cousin had come and collected all your stuff and wouldn't tell them why or leave a forwarding address. I went to student admissions and they would tell me nothing at all. I told them we were dating and they said to contact your family then and when I said I didn't know where you lived they just laughed and said well it must have been pretty serious then!

But it was, wasn't it? Serious, I mean. I mean I know we were both still freshmen and, and I don't know if I told you this at the time, but you were my first serious girlfriend. It was the first time I'd ever made love to someone, that's for sure, and I know it was yours too. Those were the days of wine and roses for me, not just leaving home and gaining all that freedom and independence, but falling in love. And I say falling in love now, even though I never told you back then because back then I thought it was too soon and I thought I would scare you off and I thought that if I could hold off saying it until maybe we were juniors, then I might have a better chance of holding on to you forever.

When we were dating, some nights as I was drifting off to sleep or in the morning just after I had awakened, I would run through a fantasy in my mind. Sometimes it was quite simple, other times quite elaborate, but always the same basic theme. I would be a professor in the business school and you would be a science professor, I could scale each of these positions up to Dean or Chairman depending on how grandiose I was feeling that day. We would either be at a small liberal arts school in the North East or at Princeton, never Harvard or Yale, though Penn some times seemed appealing. We would live on campus in a school house, sometimes we had students living with us, sometimes our own children. Always we were happy. Every time I played out these fantasy I drifted off to sleep with warm glow or started the day anew with a smile.

And then you were gone.

I kept searching for you the rest of that semester, right up to

Christmas. I would see your head bobbing along at the end of the hallway or at the bottom of a stairwell and I would race down through the crowd, knocking people aside only to find it wasn't you or lose you altogether. I would see the color of your coat through the cafeteria window and hurry past the queue thinking that finally this was it, this was the moment. But it never was.

I went home for Christmas and my parents thought I was sick. I stayed in my room most of the time. They wanted me to see a doctor, but I told them I was studying. The truth was I wasn't studying at all. My half year grades were terrible. For the first two weeks after I returned I was much the same and then I got angry. I half-wished you had died. I wished you had died because at least then I could mourn for you. At least then I would know there was a reason why you weren't there. I was angry that you hadn't left me one word, one whisper as to why you weren't there for me anymore. And now I know. Her name is Tiffany.

I can't imagine how very proud you must be of her. She is a remarkable girl, or should I say lady? Maybe everything that has happened has happened so as to lead me to her. If that's the case, then I'm OK with that. She is beautiful, she is kind, she is loving, she is patient, she is caring, she is brave and sometimes she is scared. She is you. She is the you I never got to see, but I am seeing you now through her.

You did a wonderful job raising her, she told me a little bit about it. It can't have been easy raising a child alone, but maybe you're not alone? Tiffany works hard at guarding your secrets. Maybe you married and had a dozen other

Tiffany's – though I can't imagine they're as beautiful or as special as our Tiffany.

Well I married, had a family of my own, nice house, dog, cat, horse the works. It's all gone now of course, maybe she told you that, but even then I still used to lie in my bed at night or in the morning and imagine us at that liberal arts college together or even at Princeton somedays.

With love,

Lazarus

THE EMERGENCY

IT WAS ANOTHER solitary Saturday for Lazarus Finds in the Radnor Motel.

In a moment of weakness, he had bought himself a bottle of Crown Royal at the PA state liquor store down the street, but it still sat on the dresser unopened. The muted Phillies game and the whiskey bottle competed equally for his attention, neither had won out yet. His cell phone had rung several times that Saturday, each time he had hoped it was first Tiffany and, if not, Scott Breslin, but it had always been Dick Posman. He had left it unanswered and on every occasion Dick left a message which Laz had deleted without listening to. He didn't want to hear Dick's apology, no matter how groveling. Once or twice, feeling weak and vulnerable, he was tempted to call Mary. He didn't know why, someone to talk to seemed better than no one; though she would probably be with Aubrey and he would just make a bigger fool out of himself than he had already. The Phillies were down six nothing in the bottom of the eight. Who am I fooling thought Laz?

He took a glass from the dresser and unpeeled the paper wrapper from around it. He removed the Crown Royal from its lush, protective purple velvet bag. His mouth was salivating, he could almost taste the whiskey, the rich burning impact of it on his tongue and throat. He could still just have one and he would be alright, he told himself. He cracked open the bottle and poured an inch of the golden amber liquid into the plastic glass. He added another inch and tossed the bottle cap on the dresser. The oaky aroma hit him right away and immediately transported him back to the Brandywine Room and those smokey evenings with Dick and Aubrey.

Ah, those were the days, he thought; every night, the same old thing, good food, fine drink, talking business with fellow members, arguing politics, getting drunk, going home and trying to remember any of it the next day. Then doing it all over again. Those were the days. Were those the days, were they? Lazarus thought. Well they were better than the days I have today he reminded himself.

The Mets scored a bases-loaded homer and it was ten-nil. "Chances of me throwing out that pitch are pretty slim now!" Laz snorted aloud. He raised the glass to his lips. "Cheers, world!" he said to no one in particular just as his phone rang. "Screw you Dick, can't I even have a drink in peace?" He looked at the iPhone, the display read 'Tiffany'. He ran to the sink in the bathroom and threw the scotch down into it, then he tossed the cup into the wastebasket. The ringer sounded again. He grabbed the bottle of Crown Royal, quickly screwed the top back on and shoved it in a drawer under his shorts along with the purple bag, slamming the drawer shut. The phone had finished its fourth ring by the time he picked it up.

"Hello?" he said out of breath. "Laz, here..."

"Laz, thank God!" said Tiffany. "I thought maybe you weren't there."

"I'm here... what's wrong?" he panted. "Are you OK?"

"Yes, I'm fine," she assured him. "But I need some help down here."

"Sure, what do you need. Money? I have a little on me, but I can get some more from the ATM." Laz offered.

"No, I need you!" implored Tiffany.

"Me?" said Laz. "What for?"

"Oh, it's been a disaster," the girl explained, "we've had three people call in sick tonight for the dinner service and I just don't have enough bodies to serve. I need you down here."

"But I can't do that!" exclaimed Laz.

"Of course you can," she laughed, "there's nothing to it. You saw them do it the other day."

"But they were so slick, so smooth," he pleaded. "Surely you can find someone else?"

"I'm pulling out all the stops. I've tried everyone on our emergency list. What else are you doing?" Tiffany demanded.

"I'm watching the baseball" he told her.

"It's ten nil in the ninth for gosh sakes!"

"Oh" said Laz. She knows baseball he thought.

"Dad?" said Tiffany. "See, I'm using the Dad card now. I need you."

"OK…" said Laz reluctantly, feeling deep inside that it was a long time since a of his daughter ever asked him for anything other than a new horse. "I can be there in half an hour."

"Great!" she replied. "Hurry."

By the time Laz arrived at St Jude's House, twenty five minutes later, the dinner crowd was walking in. He nervously parked the Audi right outside. Joshua greeted him immediately. "Hey Mr F, Miss Tiffany says to go right through to the back," he told him.

"Thank's Joshua," said Laz and then tossing the big man his car keys added "say Joshua, you wouldn't mind watching my twenties for me would you. I won't have it for much longer?"

The man beamed. "Sure thing Mr F, I'd be honored."

Lazarus made his way back to the kitchen, it was hot and crowded in there and he barely recognized Tiffany with an apron on and bright red scarf covering her head.

"Laz, over here, I'm going to put you with Darlene, she's from the Church of the Good Shepherd in Ardmore and volunteers here every month or so. She knows the ropes." Tiffany beckoned to a middle-aged woman. "Darlene, this is Lazarus, can you look after him please?"

Lazarus surveyed Darlene. She had the physique of an ice pick and seemed to have just about the same amount of charm.

"Lazarus, that's Jewish, isn't it?" she asked him coolly.

"Um, yes it is Old Testament," agreed Laz. "My parents were biblical scholars. But we were raised Catholic."

Darlene just gave him a frosty stare.

"My sister's called Rebekah," Laz admitted, hoping it would help.

"If they knew the Bible," Darlene advised him "you'd think they would have given you Catholic names."

"Um, I think it's still allowed." suggested Laz.

"Let's get on, they'll all be crawling in here in a minute," the ice pick told him.

"Right!" agreed Laz, rubbing his hands together much like his lawyer had taught him.

"So they get one scoop of each, no more, OK?" Darlene indicated the four pots in front of him. "Someone else will do the soup. I'll do the stew. You do the potato and the veg. Got it?" She looked to him for confirmation.

"OK" he agreed.

"One scoop, no more! Understood?" asked the ice queen.

Laz held the scoops in front of him like weapons. "One scoop, one scoop only!" he confirmed.

"Don't give them too much. They'll always be trying for more. They're cunning little so-and so's..." Darlene took him into her confidence.

"Really?" asked Laz. "But they're hungry."

"Nonsense!" said Darlene. "After this they'll all be down to McDonalds for a Happy Meal probably! Also," she continued, "if they give you any lip, give them less; if they're rude, give them less. Under no circumstances give seconds. Have you seen the size of some of these people? How can they claim to be hungry being the size they are?"

"You really seem to have it worked out..." Laz suggested.

"I've been doing this a long time." Darlene cracked an icy smile. "Oh, another thing, if they are vegetarians, do not give them extra veg instead of meat!"

"Why ever not?" asked Laz.

"Well first off," confided Darlene, "there may not be enough to go around. But second, and most important," she leaned in to whisper, "it probably means they're Muslim."

Just then a tall middle aged black woman joined them.

"Lordy, Lordy!" she said. "What do we have here, the Ice Maiden and the Ice Maiden's apprentice?"

"Oh it's you?" said Darlene, the disappointment clear in her voice.

"It is I indeed, come to your rescue in times of need." she laughed. "How are we set up here?" She looked at Darlene.

"He's doing the veg and the potato and I'm doing the stew."

She turned to Laz. "You been here before honey?"

"Er no," answered Laz. "Well I did watch the other day, but I didn't do anything."

The black woman turned to Darlene. "Well aren't you the fine one, you got new boy here doing all the work while you stand there with one hand shoved down your pants!"

"Well I..." Darlene flushed as much as a bleached white person can flush.

"Don't fret it, we all have get our thrills somehow," she winked at Laz, he smiled back. "This isn't going to work. What is your name, by the way?"

"Laz," he told her.

She reached out her hand. "Bobbi" she said and moved him to the left hand side. "You stand here and do the soup.

Serve one ladle into each bowl. It's garden vegetable, made
in vegetable stock, so everyone can have it. I'll do the
potatoes and veg and the ice queen can do the stew. Now
let's roll."

And so it went. At first Laz was slow and clumsy and
sometimes he didn't understand what people were saying to
him, so Bobbi translated the language of the street and he
slowly got the rhythm and the hang of it. The tipping point
came as he served an order of soup and a friendly voice
accosted him. "Hey, my man Mr F." It was Scratch.

"You know this man?" asked Bobbie.

"Sure thing, Bo!" confirmed Scratch. "Mr F is one of my
best customers!"

Laz tried to protest, but Scratch was headed off down the
line. Bobbi was looking at him quizzically and Darlene's
jaw was fully dropped.

The ninety minutes of food service went quickly, but by the
time the washing up was done Laz was exhausted. He said
his goodnights to the folks in the kitchen and picked up his
keys from Joshua who told him he rubbed a damp cloth
over the Audi but refused to take any money for doing that.

Tiffany was waiting for him at the door. "So?" she asked
him.

Lazarus thought for a second, then looked her in the eye. "I
really liked it," he told her. "It made me feel..." He couldn't
quite find the right word.

"Good?" the girl suggested.

He thought for a moment more. "Yes, good, but more... It made me feel 'needed'." He reached out and placed his hands on her shoulders. "And I haven't felt needed in a long time."

"Yeah" she said smiling, "That's a nice feeling."

She leaned forward and kissed him. "Good night Laz. You did good!"

THE CALL

LAZ HAD BEEN up early on the Sunday morning and had slipped out to get the New York Times. He'd made some coffee in his room and sat there ploughing through his favorite sections, reading the editorials, skipping the gloating report on the Phillies Mets game. He hadn't felt this good in weeks, months even. It was a great day to be alive. Maybe he would drive up to Valley Forge this afternoon and take a walk,. Perhaps stop at Whole Foods or Trader Joe's in Devon and take a little picnic for himself. He thought about inviting Tiffany, but decided he should give her some more notice. Maybe next week? Even four or five calls from Dick hadn't put him off his stride and he had mastered answering the call and hanging up all in one swift motion. Stephen would be proud of his thumb swiping technique, he thought.

By eleven o'clock he was feeling hungry and the coffee, necessarily black for the powdered creamer they left in your room was horrible, was starting to play havoc with his system. He thought he would just slip down and get some eggs from Minella's diner across the street. He gathered up half the newspaper and headed out the door. He had just closed it when an unknown assailant threw him hard up against the door and pinned him to it.

"OK you sonofabitch," the voice whispered, "don't even try to move!"

Laz was terrified. "I don't have much money," he cried, "but you can have it, it's in my pocket. You can take it!"

"I don't want your money you dumb-ass," said the voice. "I just wanna talk to you!"

It was Dick.

Slowly Dick released his hold and Laz rearranged his arms and head back into their more natural positions.

"What the fuck are you trying to do to me? Kill me?" asked Laz, as he picked up the sections of the Times that he had scattered on the ground during the attack.

"I've been trying to talk to you!" cried Dick.

"Then just call me!" advised Laz, preparing to walk off.

"I have called you a hundred times, you know that you idiot!" shouted Dick.

Laz headed off down the corridor. "I don't want to hear your groveling apology!" he shouted back at him.

"I wasn't calling to apologize, asshole," Dick yelled back. "I was calling about your letter to Yours Mutual from Pinkerton times three and fucking Smythe..."

Laz stopped walking and stood still for a good three seconds. He looked over his shoulder at Dick. "Have you had breakfast yet?"

"Yes," Dick shrugged. "But, I could always do with a another one..."

Across the street and in the diner they handed the menus back to the waitress who slowly meandered back to the pass to place the orders with the kitchen.

"So your lawyers are going to be getting a letter from Yours Mutual tomorrow..." Dick told Laz.

"Is it a 'fuck you' letter?" Laz sighed.

Dick squirmed a little, "It almost was, Dangle was ready to shift all our advertising to channels that had never run your story, thinking that viewers always watch the same channel some how. I don't think he's heard of a remote control yet!"

"So what happened" Laz probed.

"Well, a couple of us convinced him that should the events of your so-called demise get more deeply entrenched into popular culture, it could seriously jeopardize our whole new ad campaign." Dick continued "Jim Z has spent a shit load off money on this stuff!"

"Why do I have a feeling you had a hand in this?" Laz asked.

"Hey!" the lawyer protested. "I tried to recluse myself, several times, it's on the record. But maybe I did stick a finger or two in..."

"Like what?" Laz demanded

"Well, I told him the last time we met, when we had a huge row," Dick explained, "that you had told me you were going to see Oprah."

A totally bemused look came over Laz's face, then some enlightenment. "I told you I was going to go and 'watch' Oprah."

"'The words watch and see are semantics to a lawyer," Dick advised. "Anyway Dangle got his knickers all in a twist and changed his view, so that instead of screwing you to the ground we had to settle."

Laz dropped his teaspoon with a clatter. "You're kidding me?"

"But there are conditions" Dick advised him.

"Yeah right, I expected that," said Laz. "Go on."

Dick leant forward. "You see everything we did to you, from letting you go, to not paying you your death benefit, to breaking up your family, to treating one of our employees like shit, to not paying your life insurance promptly goes against the all basic tenets of this new ad campaign."

"So?" asked Laz.

"So" continued Dick. "Yours Mutual wants to compensate you in those areas, as best we can, to show that we really are the company we say we are."

"I don't want you putting my marriage back together again!" protested Laz.

"We could pay for counseling?" suggested Dick.

"No fucking way!" said Laz. "Leave that bit alone."

"OK, in that case, I'm authorized to offer you a compromise deal across all the monetary issues in question. That would be; half the severance you were due..."

"Half?" protested Laz.

"Let me continue," said Dick. "Half the death in service benefit,"

"Oh, that's quite good" agreed Laz.

"And," said Dick taking a deep breath, "half the life insurance payout."

"Fuck me" said Laz feeling dizzy. "How much is that?"

"Including the double indemnity for the accidental death?" Dick clarified.

"Holy crap," whispered Laz. "It's a lot, then?"

"It is quite a lot," agreed Dick. "All in all, it comes to $15,275,000 approximately."

"Holy shit, Breslin was right!" said Laz.

"What was that?" said Dick.

"Oh, nothing, nothing." Laz took a deep swig of his coffee and burned his tongue and didn't care.

"But there are conditions." Dick continued. "No one but you and your lawyer can know of this, not Mary, your children, no one. I suppose you better tell the IRS, but no one else. Understood?"

Laz swallowed. "Oh, I don't think that will be a problem." he croaked.

"There's more." said Dick.

""More? Conditions?" asked Laz.

"Money," clarified Dick. "Jimmy Z wants you to be our Jared"

"What's a Jared?" asked Laz.

"You know, the fat guy in the Subway commercials?" explained Dick. "Zee wants you to be our poster boy!"

"Fuck that!" said Laz scowling at the thought.

"$500,000 per annum guaranteed service contact, maximum thirty days work per year." Dick smiled, "Advertising boys have all the money."

"I'm in…" said Laz. "I'm a poster boy!"

Dick held out his hand. "Now can we be friends again?"

Laz looked at it, but didn't take it. "Not yet, but fifteen million is a start and I will pick up next time you call, but not yet."

"OK," said Dick, "and I am sorry, truly sorry."

"I know," said Laz. "In time…"

Dick nodded, then pointed to Laz's pocket. "I think your phone is ringing. Remember? Not a word…" he reminded him.

Laz pulled the iPhone from his pocket. It was Tiffany. "Hi Tiffany, Laz here. I was going to call you." he answered.

The voice at the other end was serious, but excited. "Laz?" she said. "I have something to tell you."

"OK," he answered. "Shoot."

"You know that lady you were working with last night?" she asked him.

"What? Darlene?" he answered. "The ice pick – Boy she was a piece of work."

"No Dad, the other one…"

"Bobbi? Yeah sure. Why? Is she OK" he asked.

"She's fine Dad" she told him. "But Bobbi is Roberta, Laz."

"So? Is she on next Saturday? She was nice. I was actually thinking of coming back." Laz shrugged his shoulders at Dick as if to say I don't know what's going on.

"She's my Momma, Laz!" Tiffany started to cry at the other end of the phone. "She's your Roberta, Dad."

Tears started to form in Laz's eyes as Dick looked on uncomprehendingly. "That was Roberta? That's your mother? She's my Roberta?" He stopped for a moment remembering the night before. "Why of course she is, I see it all now, her eyes, her cheeks, her smile.... Why she looks just like you!" The tears started to flow freely down Lazarus's cheeks. Neither he nor the girl could speak for a full minute.

The waitress arrived with the food order, but Dick just waved her away. "Not now sweetheart, bring 'em back in five would you?"

Lazarus gripped the table with all his might, squeezing the formica as if his life depended on it. Gradually he managed to compose himself, though he had an enormous stabbing pain in his throat. Somehow he forced the words to come out. "Tell her how lovely it was to see her after all these years," he instructed. He took a deep breath that sounded almost as if it could be his last. "Tell her she is still as wonderful as she ever was."

He could hear Tiffany weeping at the other end of the phone. He knew his own face was all screwed up. "Don't cry Tiffany, don't cry. Thank you for telling me. Do you know what a gift you have given me?"

Tiffany spoke haltingly through her tears, gasping for breath as she did. "It's just that she said the same thing about you Daddy. And she said she'd like to see you so she could tell you herself."

Laz pulled himself upright. "Yes, yes, of course. Did she say when?

"She said the usual place, tomorrow at seven. She say's it's still there."

Laz thought for a few moments.

"Do you remember the usual place Daddy?" the girl asked down the phone, almost pleading.

He slowly smiled as the memories flooded back, the nooks and crannies of his face compressing the streaming tears, and then laughed almost manically, "Yes, yes tell her I'll see her tomorrow. Tell her I'll see her at Pica's in Upper Darby at seven."

Laz looked at Dick who was smiling. "And tell her I'm buying this time. No more going Dutch!"

ACKNOWLEDGEMENTS

HAVING AN IDEA and starting to scribble down notes is the easy part, turning that into something more complete and substantial is much harder, getting those notes into the format of a final readable, and hopefully enjoyable, object of work is only possible through the efforts of many more than the idiot who had the original idea.

I'd like to thank my daughter Louisa, for inspiring me to always write another chapter every time I was about to give up. I thank my wife Erica who too often had to hear, "Shhh! Just let me finish this sentence!" and also for staying up well into many nights proofing and reproofing every edition. Jim Breslin and Robb Cadigan for all their advice on writing and publishing. I am so grateful for my daughter Lily for her final proof which discovered a major faux-pas in the story's timeline. I gratefully acknowledge her design of the cover and final book formatting too. I'd also like to thank Danielle Delaney for reading an early draft and for her encouragement, and for allowing me to use her daughter Laura's interest in the undertaking business as an inspiration.

Thank you to my friends who allowed me to use their names or bits of their personas for the characters in the book and finally everyone at Doe Run Press who have been so accommodating.

ABOUT THE AUTHOR

TIM MEGAW is a former television writer, producer, director and executive. He has travelled and worked all over the world but currently lives in Chester County,

Pennsylvania though he maintains strong links with his childhood home of Thornhill, Ontario and maintains a home in London. He is married to Erica and they have three children Jack, Lily and Louisa as well as many pets, not least of which is Jess, their Australian Shepherd, who patiently sat through the whole writing process.

Printed in Great Britain
by Amazon.co.uk, Ltd.,
Marston Gate.